THE FALLEN RING

A New Nemesis

KEY DAWKINS

ALSO BY KEY DAWKINS

The Fallen Ring Series
The Fallen Ring (Book 1)

CONTENTS

Knowing others is intelligence; knowing
yourself is true wisdom. Mastering others is
strength; mastering yourself is true power.

Lao Tzu

CHAPTER 1

Ｃity, University of London buzzed with the energy of young minds eager to explore the vast possibilities of knowledge. Among the throngs of students traversing the campus, Simon Jones walked with purpose, his gaze drawn to the vibrant autumn leaves that danced in the crisp breeze. It had been two years since the events that had changed his life forever – two years since the loss of his best friend, James Huang.

Now nineteen and in his first year at the university, he had chosen to study cybersecurity – an arena where his passion for technology could make a difference. Yet, despite his academic pursuits, he couldn't escape the veil of silence that shrouded him, preventing him from forming new connections. The silver Fallen Ring adorned his middle finger, its ancient runes etched around its rim. It was his constant companion, a source of both comfort and turmoil. Since that fateful day when he'd found it and become its chosen bearer, the Ring had whispered to him in a voice only he could hear.

As Simon settled into the cybersecurity lecture, his eyes inadvertently fell upon a familiar face: a beautiful brunette he had seen in previous lectures. She exuded warmth, and a gentle curiosity gleamed in her eyes. Layla Thompson, he recalled her name was. She was sitting a few rows ahead, and he couldn't help but be captivated by her presence.

The voice of the Fallen Ring interrupted his thoughts, its words a gentle murmur in his mind. *Layla*, it whispered, *a familiar face that draws your attention. Perhaps an opportunity for a connection?*

Simon couldn't help but smile at the Ring's observation. *Maybe*, he replied silently, his thoughts a mixture of curiosity and hesitance.

As the professor delved into the intricacies of digital security, Simon's attention remained unwavering – a testament to his dedication to the subject. But Layla's presence lingered at the back of his mind, offering a brief distraction from the complexities of his studies.

After the lecture, as his classmates chatted animatedly, Simon quietly gathered together his belongings. He watched Layla from a distance, her interactions with others seemingly effortless. His feelings of isolation deepened, and he withdrew into his familiar cocoon of silence.

As he made his way through the campus courtyard, Simon couldn't help but wonder about Layla, the intrigue of a potential connection sparking hope within him. Yet, his past sat heavy on him, leaving him uncertain about even the possibility of taking the first step. He glanced at the Ring on his finger. For now, he would simply relish in the friendship he shared with the Fallen Ring – a companion that had been with him through thick and thin. Its whispers of reassurance echoed softly in his mind, offering comfort as he navigated the complexities of university life.

Leaving the campus at the end of the day, Simon subconsciously stroked the silver Ring, its presence always a comfort. The busy London streets bustled around him, but he felt removed from the cut and thrust of the rush-hour, unable to shake a feeling that fate had something in store for him – an opportunity, perhaps, to step beyond the veil of silence and embrace the possibilities that lay ahead.

Later that evening, in his room, as he immersed himself in his books, researching security software, the Ring's whispering voice returned to his thoughts. *Layla*, it said. *She seems kind and understanding. Perhaps you should take a chance and talk to her.*

Simon pondered the suggestion, considering the possibility of initiating a conversation with Layla. The thought both excited and terrified him. But what would he say to her? How could he bridge the gap between them? *Maybe tomorrow*, he mused.

The Ring remained silent, a witness to his inner dialogue.

Simon turned his attention back to his books, but the idea kept nudging its way into his thoughts, growing on him, and a sense of anticipation tingled within him. It had been a long time since he'd allowed himself to hope for a connection with someone outside his family, and the thought of taking that step both thrilled and frightened h im.

As the night darkened, Simon drifted off to sleep, dreams of the future mingling with memories of the past. The journey ahead would bring new challenges, but for the first time in a long while there was a glimmer of hope – a glimmer that whispered of the possibility of healing, of forming new bonds and of being released from the grip of grief.

CHAPTER 2

The morning sun filtered through the curtains, bathing Simon's room in an orange glow as he woke from a peaceful slumber. Stretching, he yawned and got out of bed, feeling for the comforting softness of his Crocs with his outstretched feet. Slipping them on, he made his way to the kitchen, the enticing aroma of freshly brewed coffee wafting through the air. His mother, Sarah, smiled warmly as he entered the kitchen.

'Good morning, Simon. Did you sleep well?' she asked, pouring hot chocolate into a mug.

'Morning, Mum,' he replied with a nod, accepting the warm drink. 'Yes, I did, thanks.'

She glanced at her son, her eyes filled with maternal concern. 'You know, you can always talk to me if something's bothering you. You seem a bit distant again.'

He offered a reassuring smile, masking the complexities that churned within. 'It's just university and all. Getting used to the workload, you know.' He didn't want to burden his mother with his inner struggles.

'I understand, dear,' she said gently, brushing a hand on his cheek. 'Remember, I'm here for you, always.'

Simon nodded, appreciating her understanding. His mother's support had always been a source of strength as he navigated through life.

After a brief conversation, Simon retreated to his room. Sitting at his desk, he gazed at the silver Fallen Ring on his finger, its ancient runes catching the light. The words the Ring had spoken the previous evening crept back into his thoughts. It was always whispering different forms of advice, sometimes pushing him towards a darker path. It had done so in the past, so he had to be cautious and keep his desires in check. With such a monumental power bestowed upon him, he needed to ensure that he remained steadfast.

Contemplating the immense power he possessed, Simon couldn't help but feel the weight of responsibility. 'Am I living up to my true potential?' he asked aloud, engaging in a silent conversation with the Ring.

The Ring's response was dubious, open to interpretation. *Your potential is vast, Simon. Embrace it, and the world will be at your fingertips.*

He understood that the Ring could be both a blessing and a curse. He would have to rely on his own sense of morality to make the right decisions.

As nightfall descended upon London, the Fallen Ring's voice echoed in Simon's mind once more. *Shall we defend our city tonight, Simon?*

A determined glint sparkled in his eyes as he donned the dark purple liquid-like substance that clung to him like a protective suit. His muscles rippled and luminous purple eyes stared back at him in the mirror – a testament to the power he wielded.

'Yes,' he replied out loud, his voice resolute. 'It's time to make a difference.'

Stepping into the night air, Simon felt the city's pulse, the vibrations of life and energy all around him. With each stride, he embraced his destiny as the defender of London, using his powers to protect the innocent and stand against those who would harm them. As he patrolled the streets, racing across the rooftops, the Fallen Ring's whispers guided him, reminding him of the potential he held within. Enriched with a sense of humility and determination, he ventured forth, ready to face whatever challenges the night had in store.

CHAPTER 3

High in the picturesque but perilous mountains of Eastern Europe, where the jagged peaks pierced the skyline, Viktor Nemesis jogged with the grace of a predator. His thick, curly hair, the colour of midnight, flowed down to his shoulders as he moved with unmatched fluidity. The crisp mountain air invigorated his senses, heightening his connection with the untamed wilderness around him.

His piercing blue eyes scanned the rugged landscape with an almost feral intensity, seeking out prey. What had started out as an evening run had turned into a hunt as he caught the scent of a hoofed animal. Nearby, a magnificent deer grazed peacefully, unaware of the danger that lurked in the shadows.

Silently, Viktor slid like a spectre, a ghost among the rocks and trees, as he stalked the majestic creature. He possessed the grace of a tiger on the prowl, the cunning of a predator evaluating its quarry. His every step was deliberate, blending into the wild tapestry of nature. In the hush of the mountain air, he could sense the deer's every movement. Hunkering down on all fours, he primed himself, tensing his muscles, ready to pounce. He knew he could easily take its life – but on this occasion he chose not to. He didn't need to kill the deer to assert his position at the top of the food chain. Instead, he observed the mammal from a distance, a demonstration of his place in the hierarchy of the wild. Rubbing at his necklace made from the teeth of the world's top predators, he had proven his sentiment.

With a sense of dominion over the land, he returned to his remote home – a sanctuary nestled amidst the mighty mountains. A tranquil lake greeted him, its clear waters reflecting the surrounding peaks like a mirror to the heavens. Shedding the weariness of his exertion, he stood beneath the cascading waters of a waterfall, allowing his powerful physique to relax under the pristine stream, the tranquil serenade of falling water providing a moment of introspection.

As the cool droplets caressed his skin, his mind drifted to his Fallen Ring – the source of his immense power. Unlike the teenager who now conversed with the Ring, Viktor had long silenced it. When he'd first acquired the Ring, its voice had been a guiding whisper, but over time, his connection with it had deepened. He had become one with it, forming a symbiotic relationship that transcended the mere act of wearing it.

His philosophical musings intertwined with the teachings of Nietzsche – an embrace of the *Übermensch*, the Overman. Nietzsche's words had resonated with him, shaping his perception of the world and his place in it. To Viktor, the *Übermensch* was not just a concept; it was an ideal to be embodied: an apex predator that rose above the limitations of humanity and of conventional morality. His beliefs had been forged over the years, a result of the fusion between the Ring's alien power and Nietzsche's profound insights. He envisioned himself as a ruler, a force capable of bending reality to his will, and shaping the world according to his vision. As he delved deeper into his thoughts, contemplating existence and the nature of power, he drew parallels between his own journey and that of the long-extinct barbary lions of the Maghreb. They had once been the kings of their domains, just as he envisioned himself ruling over modern society.

In this moment of solitary meditation, an unexpected sensation rippled through Viktor's consciousness. It was as though an echo was resonating from afar, an energy he had never encountered before. He focused, reaching out towards the intangible signal transmitting through space, and there he sensed another Ring bearer – Simon Jones – dwelling in a distant land to the west, in a country called England.

Viktor stiffened, his eyes growing larger. He had long believed himself to be the sole possessor of such power, but had he been wrong? Was he not alone in wielding a Fallen Ring? His eyes narrowed, a spark of curiosity igniting within him. A world with multiple Ring bearers presented an opportunity to challenge his own beliefs, and to witness the diversity of human nature when granted such immense power. Who was this other Ring bearer? What challenge or threat might he present?

With purpose, he set his sights on England, specifically its capital – a realm brimming with opportunities for him to exert his influence and assert his dominion. He raised his hand. The Fallen Ring pulsed green with anticipation, sensing the path ahead – a path that would lead him to an encounter that would change the course of both his and Simon's destinies.

Change was in the air.

Chapter 4

T he city of London, draped in shadows and speckled with the faint glow of streetlights, became Simon Jones's playground as the darkness of night embraced him. Clad in his dark purple, liquid-like armour, he prowled the rooftops, moving with the speed of a silent phantom.

As he kept a watchful eye on the streets below, Simon's heart sank. A young boy was walking alone in an empty alley. While he observed from a distance, his vigilant gaze locked on the child, his keen senses picked up on an unsettling sight: a trio of foreign men emerging from the shadows. Two white men and one black man were closing in on the young boy, their intentions menacingly clear. Simon's grip on the edge of the rooftop tightened as he prepared to intervene, to be the shield of protection for the innocent.

The three men exchanged words with the boy, who seemed fearful and confused. Without warning, they snatched him and dragged him towards a blue car at the side of the road.

With a leap of faith, Simon descended from the rooftop, his armoured form landing before the men, towering above them. Lurking at the edge of his consciousness, the Fallen Ring tempted him with an array of conflicting emotions and desires, urging him to unleash his full power upon the criminals: to cripple them within an inch of their lives. But he would not succumb to the darkness; he had chosen a different path, one of restraint and justice.

The first man, driven by a mix of desperation and malice, lunged at Simon with a punch. Simon effortlessly dodged the attack, his movements fluid and precise. With a retaliatory strike, he delivered a powerful blow to the man's gut, sending him crashing to the ground.

The second man brandished a knife, his eyes gleaming with sinister intent. He sprang towards Simon, the blade glinting in the dim streetlights. But Simon, quicker than any eye could follow, grabbed the man's wrist, twisting it with enough force to disarm him without causing severe harm. Then, with the prowess of a seasoned martial artist, he executed a deft Judo throw, leaving the man unconscious as he hit the ground.

The third man rushed at Simon from behind, attempting to catch him off guard. But the Guardian was ever vigilant. With a swift back kick, he sent his assailant sprawling backwards. The man crashed into a wall near a stack of rubbish bags, leaving behind a cloud of dust and debris.

As the criminals lay subdued on the ground, the child looked up at Simon, his eyes wide with a mixture of awe and gratitude, then turned on his heel and ran, seeking safety.

Simon's heart swelled with both relief and acuity. He had made a difference to the child's life; he had saved him from a fate possibly worse than death.

The Fallen Ring's whispers intensified as the adrenaline surged through Simon's veins. It urged him to take his vengeance upon the criminals – to make them suffer for their wicked deeds. But he would not give in to the darkness; he would not let the Ring's bestial side turn him into a monster.

Not again.

Hearing subtle movement behind him, Simon swiftly turned his attention to the first man, who was attempting to rise. With a measured force, he delivered a powerful but non-lethal blow, incapacitating him while still showing restraint.

The third man lay injured on the ground, his bravado replaced with fear. 'Who ... who are you?' he stammered, bloodied and defeated.

Simon's voice was unwavering, resonating with authority. 'A Guardian. A protector of this city. A force you do not want to cross again.' His words hung in the air as he stood tall and resolute, the Fallen Ring's dark energy still humming beneath his armoured exterior. The night belonged to him, and he would meet it with unwavering courage and resolve.

Distant sirens wailed, a reminder of the city he protected. Simon's thoughts flicked to Marcus Crawford, the crime boss he had confronted twice, first while alive and then as an evil undead. Memories of those intense battles flooded his mind, and he reminded himself that he was not a comic book hero; he was merely a young man trying to atone for his past actions in his own way. Trying to find a path to complete redemption. He remembered the day he'd first encountered the Fallen Ring – the day his life had changed forever. He had been a naïve college student living a carefree life, unaware of the dangers that lurked in the deepest of shadows. But fate had had other plans for him, and his encounter with the mysterious being, Cornelius, had thrust him into a world of power and responsibility.

The Fallen Ring's whispers persisted, a constant reminder of the temptation that lurked within, of the vast possibilities he could explore. He would have to remain vigilant to keep his rage at bay, both within himself and in the city he called home.

With a final glance over the city's skyline, he whispered to the night, 'I am the Guardian, and I will protect this city from all who seek to harm it.'

And with that declaration, the unassuming Samaritan vanished into the shadows to face the challenges that awaited him in the uncharted darkness.

CHAPTER 5

Simon perched on the rooftop, the London skyline stretching before him. He'd been out here for hours, moving between the shadows, listening to the hum of the city below. His dark purple suit clung to him like a second skin, every motion effortless as he moved between alleyways and rooftops, his senses hyper-aware. His eyes scanned the streets, every flicker of movement catching his attention.

Then, his enhanced hearing picked up something - a cacophony of angry voices and footsteps. Simon's heart rate quickened. The scent of danger was thick in the air. Moving in the direction of the sound, he crawled towards the commotion. Keeping low, he found the source of the trouble. In the middle of an estate courtyard, two rival gangs were facing off, shouting insults, getting ready to throw down.

'On my life, man's got this ting patterned! Don't chat wass, fam.' A young thug in a black tracksuit paced, his hand gripping the handle of a wicked-looking zombie knife. The blade glinted under the dim orange glow of a streetlight.

'Bruv, allow it,' another snapped back from the opposing group. 'This skeng will touch man's insides!'

He could hear the crackling tension in the air, could see the way the other gang members clenched their fists, prepared for what was coming. This wasn't just a scuffle - it was about to turn violent, fast.

Simon's fingers brushed the warm metal of his Ring, its faint whisper urging him to join the fray. *Show no mercy. Show them fear. Show them pain.*

The voice was tempting, but Simon squared his jaw, resisting the urge. He wouldn't give in. Not tonight.

Dropping silently from the rooftop, Simon landed in a crouch behind a cluster of parked cars. His suit shifted, adjusting to the shadows as he crept forward.

Just as the roadmen closed in on each other, Simon moved with a speed that no one could follow, his foot slamming into the first thug's back before his knife struck the opposing man. The thug flew forward, crashing into a pile of rubbish, groaning in pain.

Both gangs froze, all eyes turning to Simon as he stepped into the circle of light cast by a flickering streetlamp. He didn't speak, and didn't need to. His very presence was enough. His dark suit making him look like a shadow come to life.

'Oi!' one of the gang members shouted, raising his hand. 'Who the fuck—?'

Before he could finish the sentence, Simon was on him. A quick jab to the face, a sharp punch to the stomach, and the thug was out cold, crumpling to the ground with a dull thud.

'Alien fuck!' another one yelled, brandishing a large machete. Simon's reflexes were too quick. He ducked low, before ramming the thug with a powerful side kick, sending him off his feet and onto the pavement with a thud, the blade skidding across the street.

Seeing this, the remaining gang members scrambled away. 'Nah, fam, we're cuttin'! Man ain't tryna get murked by some demon ting!'

As Simon was about to round up the remaining ones, the sharp click of a gun caught his attention. Guns were not common among low-tier thugs like this. He turned.

One of the gangsters, shaking but determined, aimed a Glock directly at Simon's chest. The muzzle flared - BANG.

The bullet struck home. But Simon didn't flinch.

For a split second, the shooter stood frozen, watching in horror as the bullet crumpled against Simon's suit and clattered to the ground. Simon tilted his head slightly, his piercing gaze locking onto the now-terrified thug.

'No way...' the guy whispered. 'No fuckin' way.'

Before the shooter could even think about running, Simon was on him, gripping the gun and twisting it out of his grasp. A swift uppercut to the stomach, followed by a smack to the head and the thug hit the ground, out cold.

The fight was over. Some of the gang had managed to escape, but a few lay sprawled across the pavement, groaning.

Simon took a step back, surveying the scene, then quickly pulled loose rope from a discarded stash nearby, binding the beaten roadmen. By the time he was done, distant sirens howled through the night. He glanced up as a police car turned into the estate, blue lights washing over the scene.

A concerned citizen must have called them, he thought. Good.

With one last glance at the fallen criminals, Simon vaulted effortlessly onto a fire escape, disappearing onto the rooftops as the shadows swallowed him whole.

Chapter 6

The night had been eventful, as always, and Simon Jones, the Guardian, returned home through the open window of his room with a sense of accomplishment and weariness. The dark purple liquid-like substance that adorned his body receded, revealing his ordinary clothes: a denim jacket and ocean-blue jeans. He moved gingerly, careful not to disturb his mum and his younger sister, who were sleeping peacefully in their beds. His heart raced from the adrenaline of his nocturnal escapades. The memories of the night's encounters with the criminals and the Ring's persistent whispers lingered in his mind. He had done good, but the battle between his conscience and the dark desires of the Fallen Ring was unrelenting.

Easing the window shut behind him, he sat down on the edge of his bed. The glow of the moon filtering through the curtains filled his room with a dim light, casting soft shadows on the walls. He ran his hand through his short hair, his thoughts a whirlwind of emotions and questions. The silver Ring on his finger was a weight – a constant reminder of the responsibility he carried on his shoulders. It was a power he had never asked for, a gift or a curse –

depending on the choices he made. The Fallen Ring's dark energy ebbed away, leaving him to find solace in the stillness of his room.

He thought about his mum and his sister, the pillars of support in his life. They were blissfully unaware of his night-time activities, and he preferred to keep it that way – for their sakes and his own. There was already enough to worry about in their own lives; they didn't need to bear the burden of his dangerous alter ego. And there was his search for a part-time job, a task that had proven more challenging than he had anticipated. He had applied for various positions, hoping to find something that would fit around his nocturnal responsibilities as the Guardian of the night, but so far, luck had not been on his side.

The Fallen Ring's whispers, though restrained for the moment, echoed in the recesses of his thoughts, tempting him with the prospect of using his powers for personal gain, bending the rules to his advantage. But he knew better. He knew where that path led: through the murky darkness and into a void of moral ambiguity. He sighed, the weight of the city's troubles a heavy burden on his shoulders. London was a vast and bustling metropolis teeming with life, but it also had countless threatening shadows that needed a guiding light.

Leaning back against his pillows, his mind wandered to Marcus Crawford, the criminal boss who had brought devastation to his life. The memory of their confrontations, both in life and Crawford's undeath, still haunted him. It was a battle that had pushed him to his limits, a fight not just against an adversary but also against the fury within himself.

The evening's exploits finally took their toll, and a sense of peace and fatigue washed over him. The Fallen Ring's dark energy had dissipated for now, allowing him a moment of respite. In the tranquillity of his room, he found comfort in knowing that he was not alone in his struggle. His family provided the love and support he needed, and he had also formed an uneasy bond with the mysterious Fallen Ring—a bond that carried both power and responsibility – a duo he was keen to master.

As Simon's thoughts swirled with the gravity of his life, a sudden jolt surged through him, an otherworldly presence that seemed to breach the boundaries of his mind. It was as though a third entity was creeping into his head. It was a vivid vision, a call from another bearer of a Fallen Ring, distant yet somehow close. The stranger's voice echoed in his consciousness, probing him with unsettling questions.

'Who are you, boy?' the voice inquired, its tone a mixture of curiosity and authority. 'Why do you hold back? Embrace the depths of power within the Ring. Embrace your true potential.'

Simon's heart pounded in his chest as he grappled with the intrusion. The realisation that there was another like him, a bearer of a Fallen Ring from a distant land, sent shivers down his spine. Was it possible? Could this enigmatic figure be real, or was it all a product of his weary mind?

'I ... I don't know who you are,' Simon stammered, trying to collect his thoughts. 'And I won't let you influence me. I know the dangers that come with the Ring's power. I will not let it consume me.'

The Ring bearer's voice was both alluring and unsettling, coaxing him to tap into the full extent of his abilities. 'Think of the possibilities, Simon,' the voice continued. 'Together, we could reshape the world, change it into a place of true power and order. The world as it is does not concern you nor I. But imagine how it could be. Unless you would rather a mundane existence?'

Fear mingled with uncertainty in Simon's heart. He had always known that the Fallen Ring held unimaginable power, but the idea of fully embracing it was like dancing on the edge of a precipice. The allure of unparalleled strength contrasted sharply with the consequences that could follow.

The intruder's presence persisted, delving into Simon's deepest fears and desires. It was as though the stranger was reading his very soul, uncovering his vulnerabilities.

'Who are you? Why are you doing this?' Simon demanded, his voice trembling with a mixture of anger and anxiety.

The response was a cold, haunting laughter that echoed through the recesses of his mind. 'I am Viktor Nemesis, and I am the embodiment of true power. The *Übermensch*, reshaping reality as I see fit.'

Viktor Nemesis. The name etched itself into Simon's mind like a haunting refrain. The implications of another Ring bearer, one whose intentions contrasted sharply with his own, chilled him to the bone.

As quickly as the presence had arrived, it withdrew, leaving Simon bewildered and uncertain. The room fell silent once more, and he was left with only his thoughts as he grappled with the truth of what he had experienced.

'Was it all a dream? A hallucination born from the Ring's dark energy?' he pondered aloud, desperately trying to make sense of the encounter.

But there were no answers, only the haunting laughter of Viktor Nemesis lingering in his mind. Simon's emotions boiled within him – anger, confusion and fear intertwining in a tumultuous storm.

With a surge of frustration, he shouted into the void of his own mind, 'Get out of my head! I won't be swayed by your temptations!'

Yet, as his words echoed through the silence, the laughter of Viktor Nemesis echoed in response, leaving him grappling with the unsettling truth: he was not alone in his role as a bearer of a Fallen Ring.

Taking a deep breath, he steadied himself and his heart rate slowed, returning to normal. The encounter with Viktor Nemesis had left him shaken and feeling that his life was about to take another unexpected turn – a turn that could change everything. His mind was a whirlwind of thoughts, each one vying for his attention. Knowing there was another Ring bearer, one who embraced the full extent of the Fallen Ring's power, left him questioning everything he had come to believe about his role in the wider world.

Could there be others like Viktor Nemesis? Were they all drawn to the Ring's power like moths to a flame? The realisation that he might not be the only one with these abilities filled him with a sense of trepidation and curiosity.

A creak from his bedroom door drew him out of his thoughts. Peering around the door was his younger sister, Tessa, her eyes wide with concern. 'Simon, are you okay? I heard you shouting,' she whispered.

His heart skipped a beat as he quickly composed himself. 'Oh, Tessa, I'm sorry if I woke you. It was just ... a bad dream, that's all.'

Tessa stepped into the room, her eyes searching his face for any signs of distress. 'Are you sure you're okay? You sounded really upset.'

Simon forced a smile, not wanting to worry her further. 'I promise. It was just a silly nightmare. Nothing to worry about.'

She seemed unconvinced but nodded, still wearing a concerned expression. 'All right, if you say so. Well, try to get some rest now, okay? You've got uni tomorrow.'

Simon nodded, grateful for the distraction from his turbulent thoughts. 'Yes, I know. Thanks, Tessa. Goodnight.'

She pulled the door shut behind her, and he was left alone in the dimly lit room once more. He sank back onto his bed, his mind returning to the encounter with Viktor Nemesis. The questions remained, gnawing at him like an itch he couldn't scratch. What did Viktor want? Why had he reached out to him? How long had he been a Ring bearer? And – most importantly – what should he do now?

CHAPTER 7

— · —

In the hallowed halls of City, University of London, Simon was immersed in a seminar on cybersecurity. The lecturer's words engrossed him, and he absorbed the knowledge like a sponge. He had always been a diligent student, and today was no exception. As the discussion explored the intricacies of network security and data protection, Simon's analytical mind was fully engaged.

The lecturer posed a challenging question to the seminar group, and Simon's mind raced to formulate a response, eager to demonstrate his understanding.

'Let's assume we have a critical database server storing sensitive information for a major financial institution,' the lecturer began. 'What security measures would you implement to safeguard against potential cyberattacks and data breaches?'

Simon's hand shot up instinctively. He took a moment to gather his thoughts before speaking. 'In such a scenario,' he said confidently, 'I would first recommend implementing multi-factor authentication to prevent unauthorised access to the database server. This would require users to provide two forms of identification, significantly reducing the risk of credential theft.' He continued: 'Additionally, a robust firewall should be deployed to create a secure perimeter around the server, filtering incoming and outgoing traffic to detect and block potential threats. Regular software patching and updates are crucial to address known vulnerabilities, and encryption should be used to protect sensitive data both at rest and during transmission.'

The lecturer nodded approvingly, visibly impressed by Simon's comprehensive answer. 'Excellent response, Simon. You've covered some key security measures that are vital for safeguarding critical data. Well done.'

Hearing this, Simon couldn't stop himself from smiling, knowing all too well that among the students looking his way was his crush, Layla, who was sitting a few seats away from him. Though he often stole glances in her direction, they remained strangers – two souls existing in the same space yet miles apart for the time being.

Once the seminar ended, the mysterious vision of Viktor Nemesis re-entered his mind. The Fallen Ring's voice – the persistent whisper in his thoughts – beckoned him to probe the questions that gnawed at his consciousness. In the solitude of his thoughts, Simon began an internal dialogue with the silver Ring on his finger. *What was that last night? Who was that man, Viktor Nemesis?* he asked, seeking answers from the ancient artefact.

The Ring's voice responded with an otherworldly resonance: *He was another Ring bearer. One who is older, wiser, but also callous.*

Simon digested the information before pressing further. *Okay, but isn't there more you can tell me? Like how many Fallen Rings exist?*

My knowledge may be extensive, but it is limited to that which has been passed down through time. We were forged by Cornelius, a being not of this world, a superlunary. He crafted each Ring with its subtle distinctions, granting extraordinary power to each bearer.

Simon's brow furrowed with curiosity. *Yeah, I remember Cornelius. So, what is a superlunary then? What does that mean?*

The superlunary ones are entities beyond the mortal realm, the Ring explained. *They possess extraordinary abilities and knowledge that transcend human understanding. Cornelius, my creator, is one of them. An entity of unfathomable dimensions.*

But why are there multiple Rings? And why did Viktor reach out to me? Simon pressed further, desperate for clarity.

The Fallen Ring's voice continued to echo with ancient but ambiguous wisdom. *I cannot tell you why there are multiple Rings, Simon. We were forged for reasons beyond mortal comprehension, and our true purpose lies shrouded in the depths of time. As for Viktor, it appears he was drawn to the allure of the Ring's power, just as you were to me.*

Simon's mind raced with countless questions, but the Ring's answers were veiled in cryptic ambiguity. Frustrating though it was, he understood that some truths were not meant to be easily grasped.

As he left the seminar, Layla walked alongside him, caught up in her own thoughts. When their eyes briefly met, his heart fluttered with anticipation, but the weight of the ancient Ring's revelations kept him from engaging in conversation. He made his way to the dining hall and sat down at a table for one. He placed his backpack on the floor, his peers and all the other students in the room remaining oblivious to the colossal power that lay within him. With a sigh, he stared at the silver Ring on his finger, contemplating its origins and the secrets it held. He could not ignore the presence of Viktor Nemesis, an individual who saw the Fallen Ring as a means to reshape reality, but he also did not know what to do about him.

With resolve in his heart, Simon hoped that things would start to make sense and that his questions would be answered, even if it meant facing the shadows that lurked in the corners of his own mind.

CHAPTER 8

With lectures and seminars behind him for the day, Simon felt a sense of relief as he made his way to the building's exit. The distraction of his studies had eased his mind from the unsettling machinations of Viktor Nemesis. Determined to preserve this peace of mind, Simon planned to spend the evening immersed in textbooks and notes, ensuring that his focus remained dedicated to his assignments. As he strolled through the corridors, the craving for something sweet tugged at him, and he made a quick detour to the vending machine for a chocolate bar.

Inserting a pound coin into the machine, he eagerly retrieved the chocolate bar. Just as he was about to leave, he heard a soft voice behind him.

'Hey, you're Simon, right?'

He turned to find Layla, his crush, standing there with a warm smile. 'Yeah, that's me.' He attempted a nonchalant smile in an effort to mask his delight at the unexpected encounter.

'I thought so,' Layla continued. 'I've seen you around before, and I must say, you aced that seminar earlier. Your cybersecurity game is on point.'

Simon's cheeks flushed slightly at the compliment. 'Thanks. I try my best to stay updated on all things cyber.'

Their conversation flowed effortlessly as they stepped outside into the bustling streets of London. The city's charm complemented Layla's radiant presence, and Simon found himself feeling more at ease. They walked side by side, exchanging stories and laughter. Layla's passion for her studies and her witty sense of humour made her all the more intriguing. He couldn't help but feel a connection with her as they shared anecdotes from their university experiences. They meandered through the busy streets, Layla's eyes sparkling with curiosity as she asked more questions.

'So, have you always wanted to study cybersecurity?'

Simon nodded. It was comforting to share his aspirations with her. 'Yeah, I've always been fascinated by technology and the ever-evolving digital world. Cybersecurity is like a puzzle. You have to anticipate and outsmart potential threats.'

Layla nodded thoughtfully. 'It sounds like you're meant for this field. I'm sure you'll make a real difference out there.'

Simon's heart fluttered with gratitude. 'Thanks, Layla. That means a lot coming from you.'

The setting sun had slipped lower in the sky, casting a warm glow over the city. Layla checked her watch and sighed softly. 'I should probably be heading home,' she said with a hint of reluctance.

Simon nodded, sad that their impromptu meeting had to come to an end. 'Sure, no worries,' he replied, trying to hide his disappointment.

Layla smiled warmly at him. 'I'll see you around, Simon.' Her eyes sparkled with the promise of future encounters.

A surge of hope flooded through him and he returned her smile. 'Definitely. See you later, Layla,' he replied, hoping that their paths would soon cross again.

As Layla walked away, Simon's heart raced with excitement. He'd considered asking her for her number, but then the voice of the silver Ring had whispered into his thoughts: *Perhaps it would be best to save that for next time.*

He sighed inwardly, acknowledging the Ring's advice. *Yeah, you're probably right,* he replied, playfully chiding the Ring. *But maybe you could give a guy some privacy in moments like these, huh?*

The Ring being an ancient being, with little comprehension of human humour, simply acknowledged Simon's request with a gentle affirmation.

With newfound happiness, Simon continued his journey home. The unexpected encounter had brightened his day in ways he hadn't anticipated.

CHAPTER 9

Viktor Nemesis stood amidst the bustling crowd of Covent Garden in Central London, his eyes scanning the vibrant city environment. Despite his admiration for one of the world's capitals, he felt a sense of unease. London was unlike any other place he had encountered during his travels across the globe. Observing the people, the noise and the incessant energy, he came to the conclusion that it was not a place he liked.

The journey to the United Kingdom had been arduous, but Viktor had welcomed the challenge. With the power of his Fallen Ring coursing through his veins, he was more than human, and he hungered for even more strength. His training and meditation during the past ten years had honed his senses and abilities to superhuman levels, making even the most gruelling tasks manageable.

To reach the UK, he had walked from Eastern Europe to France, displaying physical endurance that would have been nigh impossible for an ordinary man. From there, he had swum across the Channel, a feat that would have deterred even the strongest swimmers, but not Viktor, the bearer of the Fallen Ring. With his legal documents in hand, he had smoothly navigated the borders. He could not afford to draw attention from the authorities, as this would only delay his grand plan to take control of the world. Patience was a virtue he'd mastered during his years of training, and he was willing to wait for the right moment – the moment when he would topple the governments of the world, bringing all the authorities to their knees before his might.

Standing at six foot three, and dressed in a jet-black taekwondo uniform, Viktor was a Titan among the bustling crowds of Covent Garden. His piercing blue eyes scanned the faces of the passers-by, taking note of their distinctiveness but remaining detached from their lives and concerns. London, he mused inwardly, a city of vast possibilities and hidden secrets. His mind drifted back to the encounter with Simon Jones – the other Ring bearer. The thought of another possessing a Fallen Ring intrigued him. It was the first time he had come across someone with a similar gift. Who was Simon Jones? And what power did he wield? Contemplating the nature of their connection, he sensed that the teenager was still somewhat inexperienced with his newfound abilities. A faint smile crossed Viktor's lips. There would be potential in this young man. But he must proceed slowly. He needed to learn more about Simon – about his intentions – and how he handled the power bestowed upon him.

But before he made his move against the teenager, he would explore London first and have his fun. After all, the city held countless opportunities for him to test and strengthen his abilities.

With a calculating mind and an air of mystery, Viktor Nemesis remained in Covent Garden, blending into the city's fabric, yet standing out as a stranger among the ordinary. The stage was set, and the game had begun.

Chapter 10

Viktor continued to explore the busy streets of London, a city that held so many secrets and potential challenges. Gripped by a pang of thirst, he went into a corner shop, but it held little appeal for him. The shelves were filled with processed foods, a stark contrast to the raw game he hunted and consumed in the mountains where he lived. Prey was abundant there, and water was something he did not have to pay for; to have to pay for such an essential resource was alien to him.

Navigating through the aisles, he found the section with water bottles, selected one and made his way to the checkout. But upon seeing a queue of people waiting to pay, Viktor's sense of superiority as an *Übermensch* took hold. Waiting in line was beneath him; he would not wait. As he walked towards the exit, a burly security guard spotted him and called out, 'Hey, you can't just walk out without paying!' The guard pointed to the back of the queue.

Viktor glanced back at the guard with disdain. He was not obliged to pay. Rules were for ordinary people. 'I have no time for this nonsense,' he stated dismissively, his eyes locked on the hustling street outside the door. Without hesitation, the security guard reached out and grabbed Viktor's shoulder in a show of authority.

Viktor's body tensed at the touch, his instincts prepared for any confrontation. 'Take your hand off me,' he said, his tone low and chilling.

Ignoring Viktor's warning, the guard placed his other hand on his arm. In an instant, Viktor's training and superhuman strength took over. With a swift and decisive move, he grabbed the guard's arm and effortlessly slammed him onto the floor.

The vicious display of violence drew gasps of horror from the customers waiting in the queue, which echoed throughout the corner shop as other customers looked on wide-eyed, their faces a mixture of fear and curiosity.

'Some people take what they want whenever they wish,' Viktor said calmly, his eyes never leaving the guard's. 'Let this be a lesson for you.'

Sprawled on the floor, the guard was too shocked and dazed to respond.

Viktor turned and left the store, his presence lingering in the air like an unsettling aura. Putting distance between himself and the stunned crowd, he continued his journey through London's streets. Without doubt, his actions had attracted attention, but he cared little for the opinions of mere mortals. He was an *Übermensch*, a superior being, and he would wield his power as he saw fit.

Walking through the crowds, he refocused his thoughts on the other Ring bearer – Simon. Inevitably, their paths would cross, and when they did the clash of their powers would be unavoidable – legendary even. Would Simon be a worthy adversary? Or would he be just another obstacle in his path to dominance? The answer would soon come, but for now he would continue to explore the city and savour the thrill of his newfound playground, marvelling at the architectural wonders and the frenetic energy surrounding him. From the historical charm of the Tower of London to the modern elegance of The Shard, London's diverse landscape was fascinating. Yet, behind the lively façade of the city, he sensed a seething underbelly of crime and corruption.

Lost in contemplation, Viktor slipped past the passers-by, who barely noticed him despite his stature and black taekwondo uniform. He blended into the shadows, a predator lurking amidst the unsuspecting prey.

The night was young, and Viktor's thirst for adventure was growing with each passing moment. He had time before his audience with Simon would take place. So, with a sinister grin, he set forth to immerse himself in the dark pleasures London had to offer.

CHAPTER 11

Simon felt a tinge of anxiety as the lecture finally drew to a close. The academic world provided a temporary escape from the weight of his double life: ordinary university student by day and vigilant protector of London's streets by night. As he made his way towards the exit doors, his mind was preoccupied with the visions of Viktor Nemesis and the mysteries of the Fallen Rings. But the moment he stepped outside, his thoughts were interrupted by a familiar face – Layla, the brunette girl from his seminar. It was almost as if they were drawn to each other, converging at the same spot in perfect synchrony.

'Hey, Simon.' Layla greeted him with a warm smile. 'Fancy meeting you here.'

Simon returned the smile, a spark of joy igniting within him. 'Hey, Layla, it's good to see you again. How was the rest of your day?'

Walking side by side, they exchanged stories about their other lectures and the challenges of university life. The initial pleasantries soon transitioned into more profound conversations about their dreams, aspirations and even their past experiences. Layla mentioned how she was currently living in student accommodation, which led to discussions about independence and the excitement of exploring a new city. Simon, however, kept his alter ego a secret, revealing only snippets of his past without disclosing the extraordinary battles he fought as the elusive defender in dark purple. Immersed in conversation, they connected on a deeper level, their personalities complementing each other like pieces of a puzzle. Layla's passion for art and literature fascinated Simon, while her admiration for his intelligence and wit bolstered his confidence. They shared laughter over common interests, and Simon delighted in the ease he felt in her presence.

They wandered across the university campus and out into the heart of the city. Time seemed to slip away, and the world around them faded into the background. The bond between them was growing stronger, and he was glad to be in her company.

The sun sank towards the horizon, painting the London sky with hues of orange and pink, and Layla's eyes sparkled like stars in the evening twilight. Simon shivered with a rush of emotions that he hadn't experienced in a long time. He was captivated by Layla's charm and her genuine curiosity, and he loved the way she seemed to bring out the best in him.

But just as they reached a moment of undeniable camaraderie, Layla turned towards him. 'I have a tutor meeting to attend. I should head back to campus.' There was a hint of disappointment in her voice.

Simon nodded understandingly. 'No worries. I hope your tutor meeting goes well.'

They lingered for a moment longer, reluctant to part ways, but the demands of their academic lives beckoned them back to their respective responsibilities.

Before they separated, Layla stopped and turned around. 'Would you mind if we stay in touch?' A hint of shyness danced in her eyes.

Simon's heart soared with delight. 'Of course not. I'd love to.'

As they exchanged numbers, the atmosphere between them became charged with the promise of a burgeoning friendship, and perhaps something more.

With a smile, Layla said goodbye, her eyes holding a glimmer of excitement. 'Talk to you soon, Simon.'

'Definitely.' A sense of contentment that he hadn't experienced in a long time settled upon him. 'Take care, Layla.'

As they parted ways, Simon's heart felt lighter, his mind shifting away from the weight of his alter ego. In that moment, he embraced the simple joy of connecting with another person, finding solace in the warmth of a newfound friendship. There was a feeling of connection. Even amidst the chaos and uncertainty of his double life, he could find solace and strength in the bonds he forged with others. With Layla's number now safely stored in his phone, he was excited about the possibilities that lay ahead.

As the evening darkness enveloped the city, Simon looked up at the London skyline with a renewed sense of hope. A wholesome feeling washed over him as the silver Ring warmed on his finger. His support network had grown by one more. With Layla by his side, whether as a friend or something more, he was ready to face whatever challenges awaited him.

Chapter 12

Disguised in the dark purple liquid-like suit, Simon embraced the freedom and exhilaration that came with wielding the power of the Fallen Ring. He bounded from rooftop to rooftop, each leap taking him further into the night's embrace. With agile grace, he traversed the cityscape like a nocturnal phantom, leaving nothing but a flicker of shadow in his wake. Each daring stunt brought him closer to a sense of catharsis, releasing the pent-up energy that brewed within him. The city's heartbeat echoed through the night – a rhythmic pulse of existence that beckoned him onward. Swinging through the air, he marvelled at how the Ring granted him abilities that once seemed unattainable, a feeling of liberation that rushed over him with each stride. It was an experience like no other.

Drawing closer to Big Ben, the iconic clock tower loomed above him, its face illuminated in the moonlit sky. The long-standing structure stood as a testament to time, a sentinel of history watching over the city. Without hesitation, Simon scaled the tower's heights, embracing the challenge with ease. From the top, he looked out over the sprawling metropolis, admiring the symphony of lights and shadows that danced before him. The city seemed both vast and intimate from this vantage point, a canvas of human existence stretching to the horizon.

As Simon stood amidst the ticking of time, thoughts of Layla – the colourful connection he had formed with her earlier in the day – came to the forefront of his mind. The memory of their conversation brought a gentle smile to his face and warmth in his heart. But his thoughts were tinged with uncertainty. Should he ever reveal his alter ego to her? The question lingered in his mind, unanswered.

'How would she respond?' Simon wondered aloud, his voice carried away by the night breeze. He imagined the potential scenarios, the reactions she might have, but none of them seemed ideal. It was a secret he guarded closely, a part of his life he kept hidden from the world, even from those he cared about.

As he mulled over the possibilities, memories of the past resurfaced: a distant but hauntingly vivid memory of Piccadilly. Simon's heart grew heavy as he recalled the time he had burst into the Grand Casino, slashing his way through hordes of armed men to find James. The pain of that moment was still etched in his soul, a reminder of the wrath he could let loose.

Lost in the sands of time, he started when the silver Ring's voice intruded into his thoughts, interrupting his internal debate.

Such a distinguished view, isn't it? the Ring remarked, drawing Simon's attention.

It is, Simon replied, the weight of his emotions momentarily set aside. *London is a city of contrasts. Its beauty and complexities intertwine, making it one of a kind.*

The Ring made a sound akin to chuckling, seemingly amused by Simon's introspection. *Indeed, and you, my bearer, are also a contradiction. A Guardian of the night, yet a young man searching for purpose.*

Simon stared out into the night, a mix of determination and uncertainty in his eyes. *I do what I can to protect this city, to atone for the past, but sometimes I wonder if it's enough.*

Simon's grip on the railing tightened as he contemplated his next moves. The feeling that something significant was looming on the horizon lingered at the edge of his senses. Viktor Nemesis's presence weighed on his mind, reminding him that he was not the only one with such power out there.

With a final glance over the city, Simon steeled himself. Challenges lay ahead, but he wasn't alone in his fight. The connections he had formed with Layla and the Fallen Ring would provide him with strength in the battles to come.

As he descended from Big Ben, a sense of resolve settled within him. He embraced the uncertainty of the night and the unknown that awaited him. For now, he would continue to walk the tightrope between his two identities.

With twelve thundering chimes, the clock struck midnight. Simon leaped into the darkness, resuming his duty as the Guardian of the city.

CHAPTER 13

— • —

V iktor Nemesis stood tall at the entrance of an elite gym near Southbank. The walls echoed with the sounds of grunting and the clashing of gloves against pads. He had read about this place and its reputation for producing skilled fighters. It seemed like the perfect spot for him to test his might.

It was places like these where testosterone soared, competitiveness thrived and dominance was established. When mobs of men got together, leaders often needed to take charge. In the animal kingdom, dominance and territory were vital for survival and for Viktor the human world was no different. He was at the top of the food chain.

Still dressed in his black taekwondo uniform, Viktor exuded an air of confidence that demanded attention. He counted the men training inside, evaluating their skill levels. Twenty-one men – it would have to do for now. He longed for a more significant challenge, but at least it would give him an opportunity to flaunt his might.

As the men took a break, Viktor seized the opportunity to make his intentions clear. He stepped boldly into the centre of the gym, locking eyes with the coach and the group. His voice resonated loudly around the gym as he declared, 'I'm looking to take on the toughest guy in this room.'

The coach, a beefy Asian man with a stern expression, stepped forward, unimpressed by Viktor's audacity. 'And who might you be?' he demanded.

Viktor's lips curled into a faint smile. 'My identity won't matter much when I'm done with you,' he replied cryptically, his tone dripping with confidence.

The atmosphere in the gym grew tense as the other men instinctively surrounded him, drawn to the challenge he presented. The coach, not one to back down, warned Viktor to leave immediately. But the more the coach tried to assert his dominance, the more Viktor's excitement grew.

Towering over the coach, Viktor pinned him with his steely glare, a sarcastic smile playing on his lips. 'During my years of training, I sought a coach who could also be my master. That was until I realised, I was in fact that master.' Viktor's smile broadened as he stood unwavering, his eyes gleaming with anticipation. He welcomed this test of his abilities, eager to prove himself as the apex predator he believed himself to be.

With a swift push kick, he sent the coach flying backwards and crashing into the wall before slumping to the floor. The room fell into a shocked silence, the other men unsure of how to react.

Viktor egged them on, raising an eyebrow and cocking his head. The men hesitated, unsure of whether to take on this intimidating stranger. But the challenge had been issued, and Viktor's presence demanded a response.

A bald man in a tank top edged towards Viktor, his eyes narrowing. 'It's all of us against him!' he yelled. 'Let's get this damn bastard for what he's done!'

In unison, the men lunged at him, their fists and feet flying with precision and force. But Viktor was in his element, moving with the grace of a predator evading its prey. His reflexes were unmatched, allowing him to easily dodge their attacks.

With every parry, counter and strike, Viktor revealed the extent of his training. Each blow he delivered carried a calculated force, enough to inflict pain but not enough to cause lasting harm. He was toying with them, testing their limits and finding pleasure in the thrill of combat.

'Come on then!' he taunted, a smirk playing on his lips.

The men gritted their teeth, their frustration mounting as they struggled to land a hit on their formidable adversary. But Viktor was always one step ahead, anticipating their moves and exploiting their weaknesses. He dispatched them with swift, calculated strikes, his movements fluid and precise. A boot to the chest. A knee to the ribs. A crunch as an elbow shattered a nose. The room echoed with the sounds of impacts and grunts of pain.

Minutes later, Viktor stood triumphant amongst his fallen opponents, their bodies sprawled across the floor like discarded playthings.

Viktor's eyes flashed with exhilaration. He had enjoyed the exercise, but it was not enough to satiate his thirst for extreme action. He chuckled darkly to himself. He hadn't even needed to fully unleash his alter ego during the fight.

The men lay groaning on the floor, nursing their wounds and bruised egos. He had shown them just a fraction of his true power, and even then they had been no match for him.

With nothing more to do, Viktor turned to the security cameras and cleanly destroyed them and the footage, leaving no evidence of his visual presence.

With a satisfied grin, he headed back out into the night, leaving behind a scene of shattered equipment and aching bodies. This was just a small step in his grand journey. He would continue on his mission, seeking out those who dared to challenge him and crushing them without mercy.

CHAPTER 14

Viktor walked the streets, still basking in the aftermath of the gym altercation, a primal hunger for more action burning within him. His senses were heightened, and the rush of power from the fight coursed through his veins. His eyes glowed a deep green. He had become more than human, an Overman, and he craved challenges that ordinary men would shy away from.

His wish for a new challenge was soon granted. Turning a corner, he stumbled across a disturbing scene unfolding in a dark alley. A woman, clearly frightened, was being cornered by a man in a scruffy raincoat. Viktor's lips curled into a sinister grin. Here was an opportunity for him to assert his dominance once more.

Silently, he approached the man from behind, his steps light and graceful. In one swift motion, he yanked the man away from the woman and threw him several feet across the cobblestone ground. The man let out a yelp of pain as he landed heavily, struggling to get back on his feet.

'You just made a big mistake, mate!' the man shouted, trying to regain his composure.

Viktor paid him no mind and turned his attention to the woman.

She looked at him with a mix of gratitude and uncertainty, unsure of what to make of the imposing figure who had come to her rescue. 'Th ... thank you,' she stammered, her voice trembling.

Viktor briefly looked her up and down, his piercing blue eyes penetrating the depths of her soul. But his interest in her was merely fleeting, as without a word he turned and walked away while the woman looked on, still shaken from the encounter.

As Viktor stepped back onto the main street, he didn't anticipate what was about to happen. At breakneck speed, a car came rushing towards him. For a split second, he debated whether to move out of the way, but then remembered what he was – an Overman, the embodiment of power. In the blink of an eye, a dark-green substance, which flowed and shifted with a life of its own, enveloped him as he transformed into his alter ego. He threw back his monstrous head, revealing rows of jagged teeth, and with a guttural roar he met the car head on.

The impact was thunderous, but, unsurprisingly, it was the car that bore the brunt of the collision, crumpling upon impact, its metal frame twisted and contorted. The driver, who appeared to use the car as a weapon, was left dazed and injured.

Wasting no time, Viktor marched over to the wrecked car. He ripped the door open with ease, revealing the man inside, the very same man he had tossed aside. The man's eyes widened in terror as he looked up at the monstrous figure before him.

'You're in big trouble now, little man,' Viktor growled, his voice low and menacing.

Before the man could utter a word, Viktor grabbed him by his throat, cutting off any attempts at a protest. The man gasped for breath, but Viktor's grip only tightened. With a surge of rage, he unleashed the full extent of his power, and the dark-green, shimmering skin of his body enveloped the man, melting him as he screamed in agony. The screams faded along with the man, leaving the street stained with the remnants of the dead, a macabre display of Viktor's wrath.

The woman who had been accosted looked on in horror, her eyes wide with terror and filled with incomprehension at the monstrous force of nature standing before her.

With a final screech of primal fury, Viktor released his hold on what remained of the man. His grotesque form receded as the dark-green substance faded away, leaving Viktor standing there once more, still breathing heavily from the adrenaline rush. He glanced at the woman briefly and then turned and walked away, leaving her to process the surreal and horrifying scene she had just witnessed.

As he disappeared into the fog, Viktor's mind was a whirlwind of emotions and thoughts. Taking a deep breath, he forced himself to calm down. His alter ego had been witnessed in its full horror. He must disappear before any unwanted attention came his way. What had the woman in the alley thought of the monster he had briefly become? Surely, she must have been petrified. In the past, he might have taken the opportunity to assert his dominance over her too, but he no longer cared. All that mattered to him now was his grand vision of a world with him sitting on the throne. That had been his original purpose – to change the world forever. He had plans that went far beyond petty violence and control. He needed to be strategic, to play the long game.

He knew he could do just that. But he also knew what would come next: the long-awaited confrontation with Simon.

CHAPTER 15

The office of New Scotland Yard hummed with the usual urgency and dedication. Detective Chief Inspector Aida Ingram was sitting at her desk, surrounded by stacks of files and crime reports. Her mind was consumed with the recent string of unusual crimes that had been mysteriously stopped during the night. Aida couldn't make sense of it, and it bothered her. She took a sip of the coffee that her detective sergeant, Riley, had brought her, hoping the caffeine would help clear her thoughts.

'Any progress, Chief?' Riley asked, finishing his coffee in one gulp.

Aida sighed and shook her head. 'No, Riley, it's all a puzzle. There's no clear pattern, no leads. It's like there's someone out there ... playing vigilante, but we can't figure out who or why.'

Riley leaned against the edge of her desk. 'You think it could have something to do with the old crime boss, Marcus Crawford? His murder was never solved, and after he went, the whole crime scene in London shifted.'

Aida considered the idea. Marcus Crawford's murder had been an enigma, and, indeed, once he was out of the picture, there had been a notable change in criminal activity. 'It's possible,' she mused, 'but it's been two years since Crawford's death. Why would someone suddenly start taking out criminals now?'

Riley shrugged. 'Maybe something triggered it. Or maybe it's someone new trying to fill the void left by Crawford. A rival, perhaps? Whatever it is, it's strange.'

Just as Aida was about to respond, her computer chimed with a notification. She clicked on the message and saw the grim details of a recent crime scene: the remains of a man found in a back alley. 'Looks like we're back to work,' she said, her face growing serious.

Riley nodded, and they headed out of the office.

As they made their way to the crime scene, Aida's mind was still preoccupied with the mystery of their supposed night-time vigilante. She couldn't shake the feeling that there was more to the story.

The alley was cordoned off when they arrived, and the forensics team had already started collecting evidence. Aida carefully examined the gruesome sight. The victim had been brutally assaulted to such an extent that the remains were beyond recognition. Somehow, almost all of the body had been liquefied. This was no ordinary crime.

Riley approached Aida with a notepad and pen. 'Any initial thoughts, Chief?'

She sighed, her eyes still fixed on the scene. 'It's hard to say, Riley. This is a brutal murder, that's for sure. We'll need to wait for the forensics report and cross-check our databases to see if anything at all comes up.'

Aida worked alongside her detective sergeant, questioning witnesses and collecting evidence. Could this be the work of a gang or, perhaps, a vigilante? The recent decline in overall criminal activity, the enigma of Marcus Crawford's death and the pressure to keep the city safe weighed heavily on her shoulders. What was going on and why?

***

Later that evening, back in her office, Aida poured over the evidence, trying to piece together the puzzle. The forensic reports came in and the victim was identified as a known drug dealer with a history of assault. But as for the suspect, nothing significant had been found. The victim's injuries were also a conundrum, and a legitimate cause of death couldn't be recorded. Aida was stumped, seemingly at another dead end.

'Chief,' Riley called from the doorway, 'you won't believe what I just found.'

Aida looked up, her eyebrows raised. 'What is it?'

'I dug into the records from the night the Grand Casino was raided, two years ago. There were reports of a figure, a shadow-like person, spotted in the area. No one could identify him, but he was seen fighting with Crawford's gang.'

Aida's eyes widened. 'Are you saying there might be a connection?'

'It's a long shot, but it's possible.' Riley scratched his head. 'The timing fits and it might align with our vigilante theory. If he, or they, do really exist and are behind these incidents, they could be responsible for the drug dealer's gruesome murder. After all, the focus has been on criminals, hasn't it?'

Aida slowly tapped her pen on her desk, her eyes glazed. It was a wild theory, but it was the first lead they'd had in this perplexing case. 'All right, let's dig deeper into this shadowy figure. If there's any connection to these recent events, we need to find out what's going on before this gets out of hand.'

Chapter 16

London's night air carried a damp chill, the glow of streetlights bouncing off rain-slicked pavements. Perched atop a building, Simon watched the city breathe - cars crawling through congested roads, pedestrians swiftly moving through the streets and the scent of diverse foods rising in the air.

He had already stopped a handful of crimes tonight, and told himself he should head home, but the energy coursing through his veins made it hard to slow down. His body craved the hunt. Being a vigilante was exhilarating and becoming second nature.

Then he heard it.

A woman's distressed voice.

Simon's head snapped in the direction of the sound. From the rooftop, he spotted a fairly lit side street branching off a busy main road. A black BMW 3 Series sat there, its hazard lights blinking. The woman who had likely been behind the wheel was now backed against the car, two figures looming over her.

Simon narrowed his eyes.

Carjackers.

He had seen reports of a spike in stolen high-end vehicles across London, and the BMW 3 Series had been a common target. The perpetrators were getting bolder - this was happening in public, albeit in a less visible corner of the street.

This wasn't ideal. Too many eyes. Too many phones. If he went in as The Guardian, it would be all over the internet in minutes.

A more subtle approach was needed.

His suit receding back into his Ring, Simon moved fast, hopping down from the rooftop and blending into the crowd as he approached. Spotting a market stall nearby selling face masks, he ducked past, grabbed one off a rack, and pulled it over his nose and mouth. Hood up, face covered. Good enough.

By the time he got closer, he could hear the conversation.

'Just gimme the keys, love,' the taller of the two men said. His accent was thick, Eastern European, though Simon couldn't place it just yet.

'I—I don't want any trouble,' the woman stammered, clutching her handbag tightly.

The second man leaned in. 'No trouble. You hand over keys, we leave.'

Simon could see it now – well dressed, the way they carried themselves and the confidence in their stance. These were not amateurs. The taller one had his hand inside his jacket, like he had something concealed. The second guy, who was stocky, had his body angled slightly, scanning the street.

They were professionals.

Simon exhaled. He had to be fast.

Closing the distance in a few quick strides, he didn't hesitate. His feet lashed out, catching the taller man square in the ribs with a dropkick. The man grunted, stumbling back and hitting the side of the car.

The second thief reacted fast, reaching into his coat, but Simon was quicker. He grabbed the man's wrist, twisting it and forcing him off balance before driving his fist into his jaw. The impact sent him sprawling against the curb.

For a brief moment, the woman just stood there, wide-eyed.

Then the first man groaned, clutching his ribs as he rose to his feet. He spat something in a language Simon did not understand. Albanian, maybe?

The confirmation came when the second guy - who had recovered - yanked a combat knife from his waistband.

Simon exhaled through his nose. 'Knives. Of course.'

The man lunged, aiming to stab him in the gut. Simon pivoted, sidestepping as he deflected the attack with his forearm. The man was skilled, adapting quickly as he slashed again, but Simon was faster. He parried the blade, stepping in close and thrust his foot into the thief's stomach.

The knife clattered to the ground.

The first guy had recovered now, shaking off the dropkick. Instead of running, he charged Simon, throwing a wild punch. Simon ducked, twisting to the side and retaliated with a body shot to the ribs.

The thug winced but didn't go down. Instead, he grabbed Simon by the jacket and shoved him back.

Simon's back hit the car with a thud.

The Ring's energy flared inside him. *Transform. End him.*

One transformation and in one move he could finish the thief off. But Simon shrugged that thought away. He wasn't going to do that. Not again.

The thug came in once more, but this time, Simon was ready. He slipped past the man's haymaker, his little bout of martial arts training taking over. He stepped into the man's space, delivering a rapid combination - two body blows, then a palm strike to the chin that snapped the thief's head back. The man stumbled, and Simon followed up with a roundhouse kick to his head.

The thief collapsed, utterly dazed.

Simon turned to the second man, but he had seen enough. The guy bolted down the street, vanishing from view.

Simon let him go.

He turned to the woman, who was frozen in shock.

'Your keys,' he said, scooping them off the ground and handing them to her.

She hesitated before taking them. 'Who—who are you?'

Simon didn't answer. He pulled his hood lower and jogged away before the crowd could fully register what had happened.

By the time the first bystanders reached the unconscious man, Simon had already disappeared.

***

Elsewhere in London, Viktor Nemesis stood atop the hill near the Greenwich Observatory. The evening wind whipped through his taekwondo uniform, but he barely noticed it. His eyes glowed a faint green as he stared out into the distance, his gaze fixed on the horizon.

He had felt it.

The energy. The presence.

Simon was active and getting stronger.

And soon, they would meet. It was just a ticking time bomb now.

Chapter 17

The night air still had a hint of chill as Simon stealthily made his way back home. His body ached from the night's exertions, but he couldn't deny the rush he felt every time he became his alter ego, the city's elusive defender. With a sigh of relief, he reached his front door and cautiously inserted the key, turning it ever so slowly to avoid making a sound.

Slipping inside, he closed the door with a soft click and took a moment to catch his breath. He couldn't afford to rouse the suspicion of his mother and younger sister. As he tiptoed through the dimly lit kitchen, he failed to resist the temptation of grabbing a quick bite. Easing the fridge door open, he found a chocolate cake sitting invitingly on the top shelf. A small indulgence after a night of crime fighting couldn't hurt. He cut a generous slice and savoured the rich sweetness, enjoying a moment of calm amidst the chaos of his double life.

With the pleasant taste of cake lingering on his tongue, he tiptoed to the stairs, preparing to sneak up to his room. However, as he approached the bottom of the staircase, the silver Ring vibrated subtly, its voice whispering into his mind: *Someone is approaching. Shall we fade into the shadows on the wall?*

Simon hesitated for a moment, considering the Ring's suggestion, but he didn't want to use his abilities in that way. So, with a determined shake of his head, he continued his ascent, trying to act as naturally as possible. At the top of the stairs, he was met by the sight of his mother standing at the end of the hallway. Her brow was furrowed with concern.

'Simon, why are you home so late?'

Simon's heart skipped a beat as he tried to maintain a casual demeanour. 'Oh, you know, just a late study session at the university. Nothing to worry about, Mum,' he replied with a faint smile, hoping she wouldn't dig further.

Stepping closer, she placed a gentle hand on Simon's shoulder. 'You've been coming home late quite often lately. Are you sure everything's all right? You can always talk to me, you know,' she said with genuine care in her voice.

Simon appreciated his mother's concern, but it was an impossible situation. He couldn't reveal the true reason behind his late-night escapades. He gave her a reassuring nod. 'I promise, Mum, everything's fine. I've just got a lot on, with the coursework and all.' His phone pinged and a new message flashed up on his screen. It was a text from Layla. His heart skipped a beat again. Quickly, he typed his reply.

'Who's that?' said his mum, nodding towards the phone.

Simon took a deep breath, hoping to keep the conversation light. 'Oh, she's a girl I met at university. We're getting along well and have become friends.' He chose his words carefully.

Sarah's eyes lit up, and a playful smile crossed her lips. 'A girl, huh? Is she just a friend, or is there more to it?' she teased.

Simon blushed, the heat rising in his cheeks. 'Just a friend, Mum. You know me. I'm just focusing on my studies right now.' A sheepish grin spread across his face. Hopefully, his response would satisfy her curiosity.

His mother chuckled warmly, seemingly satisfied with his answer. 'Well, I'm glad you're making new friends. Just don't forget about your family,' she said, giving him a soft pat on the back.

'I won't, Mum,' Simon assured her, grateful for her understanding and support.

Bidding his mother goodnight, he retreated to the privacy of his room, letting out a sigh of relief as the door closed behind him. He took a moment to collect his thoughts, his mind still racing from the night's events.

The Ring's voice, ever present in his mind, offered a rare moment of levity. *Ah, young love. It's quite amusing to see you interact with Layla.* Its tone was tinged with curiosity.

Simon rolled his eyes playfully. *Oh, please. It's just friendship*, he replied, trying to convince himself as much as the Ring.

He lay on his bed, staring at the ceiling, replaying the events of the night and the conversation with his mother. A mixture of emotions swirled within him: gratitude for his family's love and support, excitement at the prospect of a budding friendship with Layla and a sense of duty and responsibility as the city's protector.

As he finally closed his eyes, the silver Ring pulsed gently, its power and influence a constant reminder of the world he had been thrust into. Yet, amidst the complexities of his double life, he found solace in the love of his family and the potential of newfound friendships.

Perhaps this would be the start of a successful chapter, a new beginning on an upward trajectory.

Chapter 18

A mix of excitement and nervousness swirled through him as he went to meet Layla. He had been looking forward to this moment all day, and ever since they'd exchanged numbers. She greeted him with a warm smile, and he couldn't help but compliment her. 'You look amazing today,' he said with a shy grin.

'Thank you,' Layla replied, blushing slightly. 'You don't look too bad yourself.'

They walked and talked their way through the busy streets, enjoying the crisp London air. Layla told Simon about her day and how she'd spent the last two days writing poetry, as a pastime. Simon, in turn, regaled her with some funny anecdotes from his day, careful not to mention his vigilante activities.

As they chatted, Simon suggested a coffee shop in Canonbury that he knew, so they made their way there, the conversation flowing effortlessly between them. Inside the quaint little building, the aroma of freshly brewed coffee enveloped them, adding to the intimate ambiance. Simon insisted on paying for their drinks, then they found a cosy corner to sit and chat, where they delved into deeper topics, discussing their interests, passions and even their fears.

Layla confessed that Simon was one of the few people she felt comfortable talking to in depth. 'You're a good listener,' she said with a warm smile. 'It's refreshing to spend time with someone I can be myself around.'

Simon felt a swell of pride and a genuine connection with Layla. He admired her openness and honesty, and he found himself opening up more than he had expected. The idea of revealing his secret to her flitted through his mind, but he hesitated. He wanted to trust her, but he also knew the potential danger of sharing such a secret.

As they sipped their coffee, the topic of responsibility came up.

'You know,' Layla said thoughtfully, 'I believe that making the right decisions in life takes a lot of courage and responsibility. Knowing the best thing to do each time is a virtue.'

Simon chuckled at the sentiment. 'You're right,' he said, glancing at his Ring briefly. 'But sometimes it's difficult to know how to balance that responsibility.'

Layla nodded in understanding. 'I think everyone struggles with that in their own way. But I believe that we all can handle whatever comes our way. We just have to dig deep, no matter how hard it gets.' She looked at him with a reassuring smile.

Simon nodded, his mind racing with thoughts of his alter ego and the weight of responsibility that came with it. Should he tell Layla about his secret, about the Fallen

Ring and his night life as a vigilante? But how would she react?

Before he could make up his mind, a sudden wave of discomfort seized him. It was as though something was intruding into his mind again, just like the first time. He winced, clutching his head, trying to fight off the headache that accompanied the intrusion. It was as though he was receiving a signal, some kind of intangible but tethering connection from afar.

'Layla ... I'm sorry,' Simon stammered, trying to hide his pain. 'I need to excuse myself for a moment. I'll be right back.'

Layla looked on with concern and reached out to touch his hand. 'Are you okay? Do you need any help?'

He forced a smile, grateful for her concern. 'No, I'll be fine. Just a sudden headache, that's all. I'll be back in a minute.'

Layla nodded, her eyes full of worry.

Simon quickly made his way to the bathroom. Once inside, he slumped against the sink, his mind a warzone, battling for clarity. As he gripped his temples, he noticed a glow emanating from the runes of the Fallen Ring. It was bright and pulsating. An indicator of the intensity of the episode. With images frantically flashing in his mind's eye, Simon saw Viktor in a woodland area, meditating, calling out to him.

Could he be in London? When did he arrive? The questions rushed over him, but vying for control, he steadied his breathing, becoming conscious of the here and now.

Then, just as suddenly as it had come on, the psychic intrusion dissipated, leaving Simon blank for a moment. Adrenaline coursed through his body. He splashed his face with cold water, resetting his inner focus. Viktor was indeed in England, and he now knew where. Remembering Layla, he checked his appearance in the mirror and turned to leave the bathroom.

His heart raced as he walked back to the table, trying to hide his unease from Layla. He must not involve her in whatever dangerous situation Viktor was calling him to. The visions had been unsettling, but he couldn't ignore the urgent pull he felt to Sydenham Hill Forest.

'Layla,' he said, trying to keep his voice steady, 'something unexpected has come up, and I need to sort it out immediately. I'm really sorry, but I have to go.'

Layla looked disappointed, concern evident in her eyes. 'Is everything okay?' she asked, her voice laced with worry.

Simon forced a smile. 'It's nothing serious, just a minor emergency. I'll catch up with you later. I promise.'

Though she seemed disappointed, Layla nodded. 'All right, just take care of yourself, okay?'

'I will,' he replied, grateful for her support. 'I'll see you later, Layla.'

With that, Simon quickly made his way out of the coffee shop. The visions of Viktor's forest location were clear in his mind, urging him to hurry. He didn't have much time to waste.

Outside, the city lights blurred as Simon turned down a narrow road and activated the power of his Fallen Ring, transforming into his dark-purple metallic-like form. He leaped from rooftop to rooftop, the cool air brushing against his face. Moving with speed and agility, he focused his mind on the task ahead.

The time for his audience with Viktor Nemesis had arrived.

CHAPTER 19

The sun hung low in the evening sky, casting a soft glow over the ruins of the old castle in Sydenham Hill Forest. The woodland was still and eerily silent. Not a single sentient life form stirred, but the air buzzed and clicked with static electricity.

Standing before the dilapidated structure, Simon breathed heavily, his heart racing and his Fallen Ring pulsing with an otherworldly energy. He could sense Viktor was somewhere deep within the dated structure. He couldn't afford to waste a single second. So, with a deep breath and his hand balled into a fist, he entered the crumbling castle, ready to face the enigmatic man who eagerly awaited him. The tension in the air was palpable. It had all come down to this.

Simon made his way through the ruins of the old castle, his body tingling with a surge of fear and trepidation. The humidity was suffocatingly thick, and the atmosphere intensified as he ventured further in. His Ring tingled, its ancient runes glowing softly in response to the presence of another Fallen Ring nearby. Reaching the heart of the ruins, he stopped dead. There sat Viktor Nemesis, the man who had been haunting his mind for weeks. Dressed in a black taekwondo uniform, Viktor was sitting in the lotus position, his hands clasped together, both index fingers pointing downwards. A shock of curly, black hair hung low at his shoulders, and he exuded an aura of unmistakable power and confidence. As his glowing green eyes met Simon's, a smile crept across his face.

'Ah, the illustrious Simon Jones,' Viktor said, his voice smooth and commanding. 'It's a pleasure to finally meet you in person.'

Keeping his guard up, Simon observed Viktor with caution. 'I wish I could say the same, but I barely know who you are.'

Viktor chuckled, a dark edge to his laughter. He unfolded his legs and stood up. 'But that's why we're here, isn't it? To understand each other.'

Like two opposing magnets, Simon and Viktor circled each other within the ancient ruins, the might of their powers bubbling just below the surface, ready to blow. Viktor's glowing green eyes bore into Simon's with a mix of curiosity and confidence.

'So, Simon,' Viktor began. 'Have you decided to walk the path of enlightenment? To shed all weakness and transcend humanity? To rule with an iron fist? To master this realm and bend reality to your will? To take your seat on the throne of true glory? Or, have you come to challenge me?'

Simon held his steady gaze, unwilling to show any signs of weakness. 'I'm not here to fight you, Viktor. I'm here to understand you, and help steer you off whatever dangerous path you're on. Your desire for power and domination will only bring destruction.'

Viktor chuckled, his voice low and menacing. 'Destruction? No, my dear boy, what I seek is not destruction but evolution. The world is stagnant, drowning in its own mediocrity. The weak cling to their feeble notions of morality and justice while the strong languish under the tyranny of the systems. I want to break those chains and unleash a new era of true power and freedom. We have the power to change the course of history, to shape the world as we see fit.'

Simon shook his head. 'But at what cost, Viktor? You talk of strength, but strength also lies in compassion and empathy, in using power to protect the vulnerable, not exploit them.'

Viktor's eyes narrowed, and a sinister grin spread across his face. 'Compassion and empathy are for the weak, Simon. They hold little place in the heart of an Overman. We have been gifted with abilities beyond mortal comprehension, and it is our duty to use them to shape the world. To fail to do so would be foolish!'

'But that doesn't mean we have the right to rule over others,' Simon retorted. 'With our powers comes accountability. We must use our gifts for the betterment of all, not just for our own desires. I know how it feels to wield such power, and to let it run rampant. But we must not let it.'

Viktor scoffed. 'You think running around playing an unknown hero will make the difference? That moral obligation is for those who lack the strength to seize their destiny. I refuse to be bound by the whims of lesser men.

The world will bow before me, and I will be its ultimate ruler. A true being with all his power realised. As Ring bearers, this is in our blood. The Ring on your finger calls to you. You must answer it, and together we will change the world.'

Looking deep into Viktor's steely green eyes, Simon could feel the allure of his words pulling at him. The promise of limitless power, of being able to reshape the world according to his own vision was tempting. Such a possibility could bring its advantages. But, deep within himself, he knew that such a path would lead only to darkness and chaos. He had experienced some of that two years ago, and he never wanted to go through that again.

'You're deluded, Viktor,' Simon said, his voice firm. 'Power without restraint is a dangerous weapon. It corrupts the soul and blinds us to the suffering we cause. You may see yourself as an Overman, but, in truth, you'd be nothing more than a tyrant.'

Viktor's expression hardened, and his stance became more aggressive. 'You may think you're different, Simon, but you're just as weak as the rest. You cling to your pathetic notions of right and wrong, but they will be your downfall.'

With the tension between them at its peak, they stopped circling each other. Standing still, Simon knew that the time for words had passed. It was clear that Viktor would not be swayed by reason alone. He had no choice but to face him in battle.

'If you cannot overcome your shadow of weakness then I have no choice but to kill you myself!' Viktor said, taking a step forward.

With a determined nod, Simon activated his Fallen Ring, its purple liquid-like substance enveloping his skin. Power surged through his body, and his eyes glowed with an intense violet hue.

Viktor's green eyes blazed with equal ferocity as he transformed into his alter ego, his dark-green form exuding evil menace. With a primal, rage-filled roar, he revealed his daggers for teeth.

Simon recoiled inside himself but stood his ground. Viktor was clearly immensely powerful. Their clash would be like no other. His greatest test yet.

Without further warning, Viktor lunged forwards with blinding speed, his fist aimed at Simon's face. Simon swiftly blocked the blow, but the force of it sent him stumbling backwards. Quickly regaining his footing, he retaliated with a swift roundhouse kick aimed at Viktor's head.

Viktor effortlessly dodged the attack, moving with an unnatural grace. He countered with a series of lightning-fast punches to Simon's body, each strike landing with bone-crushing force. It was as though he was being peppered by ten-thousand bullets all at once. Simon did his best to defend himself, parrying the blows with his arms and legs, but he could feel the impact taking its toll.

Their movements became a blur of motion as Simon's mind raced, trying to anticipate Viktor's next move. But it was like trying to predict the path of a raging storm. Viktor's attacks were relentless, and Simon was struggling to keep up. Ducking under a devastating haymaker, he caught Viktor with an uppercut to his face and a teep kick to the chest, but they seemed to have little effect on the formidable Overman. Viktor's beastly form seemed impervious to pain, and he continued to press forward with unwavering tirelessness. He was like a tank.

The forest echoed with the sound of their blows, the clash of their Fallen Rings sending shockwaves through the ancient castle walls. Simon's limbs were heavy with exhaustion, but he couldn't back down. He couldn't afford to show weakness, not in front of someone as ruthless as Viktor.

As the battle raged on, Simon's movements became slower, his strikes less precise. He was running on sheer willpower, refusing to yield even as his body grew weaker with every blow. Viktor was unyielding, his glowing green eyes burning with an intense focus.

In a desperate move, Simon channelled the power of his Fallen Ring, and his armour shimmered with a brilliant purple light. He unleashed a powerful energy blast towards Viktor, hoping to catch him off guard. But Viktor was prepared, deflecting the blast with a swift sidestepping motion.

With a malevolent grin, Viktor closed in on Simon, channelling energy into his own hands, enveloping them in a dark-green aura. He launched a ferocious attack on Simon, punching him square in the chest and sending him reeling backwards, crashing into the stone walls of the ruins. The force of the blow sent shockwaves through the ground, cracking the stone beneath their feet. The loose bricks came toppling down on Simon, almost burying him completely under the rubble. His body ached from the brutal assault. He tried to stand back up, but his legs felt like lead, barely able to support him.

Viktor stood over him, his chest heaving, and a sinister smile on his face. 'You're strong, Simon, but not strong enough. You hesitate, and that is your weakness. If you embraced the full power of the Fallen Ring, you could be unstoppable.'

Gasping for breath, Simon felt a surge of anger and frustration. Viktor was right. He had been holding back, afraid of the darkness that lurked within his alter ego. But giving in to that darkness could be his undoing.

'I won't become like you, Viktor,' Simon managed to say, his voice strained. 'Your quest for power is a path of destruction. I will fight to protect those I care about, even if it means facing you.'

Viktor chuckled, his grin widening. 'We'll see, Simon. Take some time to reconsider my offer. Once you've realised the true potential of your Fallen Ring, seek me out at Piel Island. I look forward to our next encounter.'

With that, Viktor turned and walked away, leaving Simon in a heap on the forest floor. The sound of his footsteps faded into the distance, and the woodland fell silent once more.

Covered by the mass of rubble, Simon lay there, weak and exhausted. He must go after Viktor and stop him before he could harm anyone else. But with very little energy, he could barely move from beneath the pile of stone.

Pulling himself up onto all fours, he gasped heavily as the purple liquid-like substance receded back into the silver Ring. With a heavy sigh, he collapsed back down again, his fighting spirit utterly spent.

Chapter 20

Viktor Nemesis stood at the edge of the water, gazing across the dark expanse towards Piel Island. Just arrived in Roosebeck, Cumbria, he had wasted no time striding to the land he wished to reside in. The events of his battle with Simon still played in his mind like an action film. It had been a satisfying confrontation, the first time he'd faced a true challenge since acquiring the Fallen Ring. The young man had shown promise, but he lacked the conviction and ambition that he possessed.

As he made his way across to Piel Island, Viktor's mind was consumed with thoughts of their next encounter. Simon was clearly conflicted, torn between the power of the Ring and the responsibility that came with it. It intrigued him no end. Perhaps he could sway the young man to join him in his quest for domination.

With each stroke towards the island, Viktor's thoughts intensified, focusing on the possibilities of their future meeting. Should he kill Simon and absorb his power, further increasing his own strength? Or should he spare the boy and let him witness his ascension to the pinnacle of power, ruling over all.

As the island loomed closer, Viktor stared into the deep, blue water, and the Fallen Ring hummed with energy, echoing the thoughts and desires that filled his mind. Immense power coursed through him, urging him to embrace his role as the Overman, the apex predator of the world.

Across the water, the wind whispered through the trees, as if the island itself was acknowledging Viktor's presence. A surge of anticipation ran through him. It was the calm before the storm, and Piel Island was the perfect place for him to gather his strength and plan his next move.

Reaching the shore of the island, he took a moment to breathe in the salty air. He felt an overwhelming sense of purpose, as if he had finally found his true calling. The Fallen Ring's essence surged within him, filling him with an insatiable desire to act on his visions. With each step he took on the island, his mind became more resolute. He would show the world what he was capable of, and those who opposed him would kneel before his might. Simon would be given a choice: to join him in his conquest or face the consequences of his defiance.

As the day turned into night, Viktor settled into a small, abandoned cabin on the island. The isolation suited him and the darkness fuelled his ambition, making him feel more alive than ever. He meditated in the silence, channelling the energy of the Fallen Ring into his hands. The green glow intensified, a symbol of his growing strength. In the solitude, he plotted and planned. He was a force to be reckoned with, a man who had the world in his hands, much like a cat that toyed with a ball of yarn.

As the first rays of dawn broke over the horizon, Viktor woke with a feeling of excitement. The world was his for the taking, and he would stop at nothing to achieve his goals. He had Simon in his sights. The next chapter of their encounter would be even more consequential.

The island seemed to vibrate with the power emanating from him, and his eyes glowed with a determination that bordered on madness. The time had come to set his plans in motion, to take the world by surprise and cement his rule as the ultimate sovereign. With a deep breath, he rose to his feet and looked out towards the horizon. Piel Island would be the birthplace of his reign, the starting point of a journey that would change the course of history. He was invincible, a true Titan, ready to conquer all that lay before h im.

He left the cabin and walked to the shore of Piel Island, the Fallen Ring pulsating with power. He had the world at his feet. The game was already underway, and he was more than ready to play it to its thrilling conclusion.

CHAPTER 21

S imon stumbled into his room, his body screaming in agony from the brutal beating he had endured at the hands of Viktor Nemesis. His breath came in ragged gasps, and every movement sent jolts of pain through his battered form. Collapsing onto his bed, he gazed up at the ceiling, his mind racing with a whirlwind of emotions and thoughts.

The fight with Viktor had been intense, unlike anything he had ever experienced before. The Fallen Ring had granted him incredible power, but it seemed insignificant compared to the overwhelming strength and brutality of his adversary. Each blow from Viktor had felt like a sledgehammer crashing into his body, leaving him reeling.

As he lay there, memories of his previous battles resurfaced, haunting him like skeletons hidden away in the shadows of a closet. He couldn't shake the image of that fateful night when he had confronted Marcus Crawford, the criminal boss who had taken his friend's life. He had been pushed to the brink that night – forced to take a life to protect the ones he cared most for. The memory of that moment still gnawed at his conscience, leaving a deep scar that refused to heal.

The encounter with Viktor Nemesis had reignited that same rage within him. He wanted to surrender completely to the power of the Ring and let his inner turmoil and burning desire for vengeance take control. It was so very tempting, but he couldn't afford to let that thought consume him. He had to be careful, to tread lightly and keep his emotions in check. The Fallen Ring's power was a double-edged sword. He must not let it turn him into a monster.

His thoughts returned to Layla. Her warm smile and genuine interest in him had touched something deep within his heart. He enjoyed spending time with her, and part of him longed to let her in on his secret life as a vigilante. But he couldn't risk her safety. The danger that surrounded him was not something he could burden her with, and he couldn't bear the thought of her getting hurt because of him.

And then there was his family, the two people who meant the world to him. His mother's loving and caring nature had been a constant source of support throughout his life, and he couldn't let anything happen to her. His younger sister, Tessa, was like a beacon of light in his often-dark world. He would do anything to protect her innocence.

The memory of James, his childhood friend, haunted him, a ghost from the past. Losing James had been a devastating blow. He could not lose anyone else. He had to be strong, not just for himself, but for the people he loved.

With a heavy sigh, he pushed himself up from the bed, wincing as his battered body protested at the movement. The pain served as a constant reminder of the consequences of his actions. He needed to get stronger, both physically and mentally.

Walking over to the mirror, he gazed at his reflection. The faint glow from the Ring's runes pulsed softly, a stark reminder of the power that lay within.

Simon, you know what must be done. The whispering voice resurfaced in his mind. *You must unleash your fury. You must tap into our core and let the fires of hell rain down upon your nemesis. If you wish to win, it is essential.*

Simon mulled over the Ring's words. He had to find a way to control the Ring's power, to use its force for good and not succumb to its dark allure. *No, we must rise above that. We must channel into our higher sense of strength. We must draw upon it and use it as fuel instead of blind rage. I know we have it in us. Just let me take control.*

Taking a deep breath, he made a silent promise to himself. He would train harder, push himself further and find a way to harness the power of the Ring without losing himself in the process. He would protect those he loved, even if it meant keeping them at arm's length.

As he stood beneath the soothing waters of a warm shower, a determination rose from deep within him. He would not let Viktor Nemesis win. He would not let the darkness consume him. He had a responsibility, not just to himself, but to everyone around him.

Leaving the bathroom, he glanced at his phone and saw a message from Layla. He felt a pang of guilt at the thought of cancelling their plans, but it was for the best. He couldn't let her get caught up in his dangerous world.

With a heavy heart, Simon sent a brief message to Layla, apologising for cancelling and promising to make it up to her soon. He could not keep his distance forever, but for now, it was the only way to keep her safe.

He sat down on the edge of his bed. The road ahead would be difficult. The final battle with Viktor Nemesis was on the horizon, and he would need all the strength and determination he could muster. But he was ready to face whatever was coming his way, to protect the people he loved and to be the hero he knew he could be.

With that thought in mind, he went downstairs and left the house. Before the inevitable standoff, he had to make an important visit.

He needed to pay his respects.

CHAPTER 22

The day was overcast and a soft drizzle was falling from the leaden sky as Simon made his way to the cemetery. He walked slowly, each step weighed down with memories and grief. The patter of raindrops hitting the leaves and the gravestones echoed in his ears, creating a sombre soundtrack that matched the occasion. It had been a year since he'd last visited James's grave, but his annual pilgrimage was a ritual he could never miss.

Approaching the tombstone, he noticed a figure nearby. A slender man in a black overcoat, his shoulders slightly hunched, was making his way towards the same grave. Simon's heart skipped a beat as he recognised the man – it was Andy Huang, James's estranged and abusive father. Memories of their past encounters flooded back, the pain and anger still fresh in Simon's mind.

Andy stopped before the tombstone, his eyes fixed on the engraved name of his son. Lost in thought, his face was a mask of sorrow and regret. For a moment, Simon felt a pang of sympathy towards the man. Maybe, just maybe, he did actually care about James in some twisted way. But the years of abuse and neglect were too deeply ingrained in Simon's memory to allow him to forgive easily.

As Andy looked up from the grave, with dark circles around his eyes, his gaze met Simon's. There was a flicker of recognition in his eyes, but it quickly faded. Andy didn't recognise him, and he was thankful for it. He didn't want to be drawn into a conversation with James's father, not on this day of mourning. Even if he were to engage with Andy, he wouldn't know where to begin. With a heavy heart, he turned away and walked back towards the entrance of the cemetery. He needed space and time to process the emotions that had been stirred up by seeing Andy again. Holding onto anger and bitterness would not bring him peace, but letting go of the pain was easier said than done.

He walked out through the cemetery gates, lost in the memories he and James had shared and the dreams they'd had for the future. It wasn't fair that James's life had been cut short. What kind of person would he have become had he been given a chance? But amidst the sorrow, res-oluteness sparked within Simon. He couldn't let the pain and anger consume him. He couldn't let the past hold him back. James would not have wanted that for him.

His mind shifted to Viktor Nemesis. The very reason he was here today, paying his respects, was because of the path he had chosen to walk. Viktor's grave ambitions, his lust for power and the threat he posed to everyone Simon loved weighed heavily on his mind.

The decision was clear. There was no running from his responsibility. He had to face Viktor and put an end to his mission, once and for all.

As he walked back up the road, and back into the world of the living, the rain subsided and a faint ray of sunlight broke through the clouds. It was as if the heavens were offering a glimmer of hope, a sign that even in the darkest of times, there was still a chance for redemption.

The die was cast. He would set out on his journey to Piel Island to protect those he loved and to put an end to the darkness that threatened to consume him and the world.

This time, he was ready to face the ultimate challenge of his life.

CHAPTER 23

L ayla sat in her small, cosy art studio, the soft glow of a table lamp casting warm light on her canvas. Her nimble fingers danced gracefully across the paper as she delicately brought Simon's features to life with every stroke of her brush. The room was filled with the faint scent of paint and turpentine, creating an atmosphere of tranquillity and creativity.

As she worked her paintbrush deftly, her mind drifted back to her last meeting with Simon. They had spent a wonderful afternoon together, walking and talking through the streets of London. She felt a genuine connection with him, as if they had known each other for much longer than they actually had. She admired his passion for cybersecurity, his sense of responsibility and his down-to-earth demeanour. But something had seemed off when they parted ways. She recalled the look in his eyes, a mix of uncertainty and sadness, when he said something had come up and he had to leave. What had happened to him? Respecting his boundaries, she hadn't pushed further.

Her phone buzzed with a new message notification, drawing her from her thoughts. She snatched it up, hoping it was Simon. Her heart sank a little when she read his message. He had to cancel their plans and wouldn't be able to meet up. She tried to hold back her disappointment, reminding herself that Simon probably had a lot on his plate, and she didn't want to burden him further.

With a sigh, she returned her attention to the portrait. Each stroke of her brush felt like an intimate gesture, as if she was getting to know Simon on a deeper level through her art. She captured the way his eyes sparkled with intelligence and kindness, as well as the curve of his smile, which made her heart skip a beat. But what was happening in Simon's life, away from their budding friendship? There was an air of mystery about him, and she had a feeling that he held secrets that he wasn't ready to share. She respected his privacy but a nagging curiosity tugged at her.

She finished the portrait with care, making the final touches to Simon's features. The painting portrayed his essence: his strength and vulnerability. She stepped back to admire her work. There was a sense of satisfaction in creating something that felt so personal and intimate. She couldn't wait to show Simon himself. She knew he would appreciate it.

As the evening wore on, Layla found herself lost in more thoughts about Simon. Was he okay? What was he doing? Maybe he needed someone to talk to. She hoped he knew she was there for him, even if they were still just getting to know each other. With resignation, she cleaned her brushes and prepared to call it a night. She couldn't force Simon to open up or share his struggles, but maybe someday he would feel comfortable enough to confide in her.

She turned off the lights and locked up her studio, silently wishing for Simon's safety and well-being. The portrait of him remained on the easel, a reminder of the connection they shared and hope for a future where they could be more than just friends.

With the image of Simon's face etched in her mind and heart, Layla headed home. They would soon meet up again. Until then, she would continue to paint, pouring her emotions and thoughts onto the canvas, and waiting for the day when their bond would deepen, and they would become closer than ever before.

Chapter 24

The atmosphere on Piel Island was charged with electricity as dark, thunderous clouds swirled above. The sullen sky crackled with lightning, and rumbling thunder seemed to forewarn of the impending clash between the two formidable foes. It was as though nature and the celestials themselves were waiting to bear witness to the epic showdown that was soon to commence.

Stepping onto the shore, Simon was enveloped by the ominous atmosphere. Unlike before, however, this time he would hold nothing back. The pulsating power that dwelled within him and his opponent would be on full display. This would be their battleground – and only one would walk away. A sense of determination surged within him. He forged ahead, approaching the figure standing at the very centre of the island.

Viktor Nemesis turned around, a wicked smile etched across his face. 'Ah, Simon,' he greeted, his voice dripping with malice. 'I see you still haven't transcended your limits. You are wasting your potential.'

Simon steadied himself. His destiny did not lie in ruthless ambition. 'No, Viktor. It is you who has been too short-sighted. Instead of transcending, you've descended.'

Viktor's eyes, now glowing green orbs, burned with a contemptuous fury. 'You're going to die here, Simon. Once I've killed you, I'll take your Fallen Ring.' He pointed to Simon's finger. 'I hope those who you hold dear will remember you.'

The storm intensified around them, lightning illuminating the darkened sky and casting an eerie glow over the combatants as they transformed into their alter egos, their forms radiating with raw energy. Taking a fighting stance, they faced off, a stark contrast of purple and green.

In a sudden motion, Viktor initiated the attack, launching a barrage of spiked projectiles towards Simon. With swift reflexes, Simon dodged the deadly tips, rushing towards Viktor in an effort to close the distance between them. Viktor leaped forward, and the two Titans collided, the ground beneath them trembling with the impact of the blow.

Their close-quarters combat ramped up as Viktor morphed his left hand into an oversized axe, swinging his deadly limb towards Simon. Back-flipping just out of range, Simon evaded the attack. He landed nimbly on his muscular legs, thrusting himself forward and catching Viktor with a quick jab and a right hook before taking hold of him by his shoulders and tossing him overhead.

Landing on the dirt with a thud, Viktor sprang back onto his feet and hurtled towards Simon. Turning his hands into razor-edged blades, Simon sliced at Viktor, piercing his midsection and slashing at his dark-green form. With an enraged shriek, Viktor sidestepped his assailant and clamped his clawed hand around Simon's throat, slamming him face down onto a boulder until the rock cracked.

Staggering from the impact, Simon turned around only to see Viktor kick him backwards and into a wooden outbuilding, splintering it in the process. Throwing off the shattered wooden planks, Simon pushed himself back up, his hands curling into fists. It would take more than that to keep him down.

Charging towards Viktor once again, Simon came in swinging, his fists blazing through the air and landing with brutal force, each strike calculated to inflict maximum damage. Viktor absorbed the blows, his sinewy form quivering with the impact.

Simon followed with a spinning hook kick, aiming for Viktor's head, but the seasoned warrior ducked under the attack. In a swift counter, Viktor delivered a powerful knee strike to Simon's abdomen, momentarily staggering him. Thrusting his elbow forward with bone-crushing force, Viktor connected with Simon's jaw, sending him reeling. As Simon struggled to regain his footing, his opponent closed in, tackling him into the wet grass, pinning him down. Locked in a fierce struggle, they rolled and grappled with each other.

Seeing an opening, Simon, mid roll, threw his arm around Viktor's throat and wrestled his way behind him, taking his back. Wrapping his massive limbs around Viktor's head, he squeezed hard, choking Viktor. But his hold was short-lived. Jagged tendrils shot out from Viktor's spine, skewering him. Gripped by agony, Simon fell to his knees, clutching his aching body.

Viktor turned and stood up, straightening to his full height, tendrils flailing from his back. With a snarl, he flung his spiked hand at Simon, backhanding him a few feet away. Crashing onto his back, Simon lay on the grass, nearly drained of his spirit. As he craned his neck up, he wheezed as Viktor drove his heel into his chest, threatening to fracture his ribs. Howling in pain, Simon felt the pressure ease as Viktor removed his foot and hoisted him up above his shoulders.

'You may be imbued with the Ring's power, but with or without it, you are merely a young man, whereas I am a deity!' Viktor declared, holding Simon high above his head.

With his arms limp at his sides, Simon was thrown into an abandoned cabin, flattening the structure upon impact.

Fatigued, he lay on his back, gasping for breath, his body bruised and battered from the relentless onslaught of Viktor Nemesis. The malevolent figure stood above him, a wicked grin etched across his face, revelling in his apparent victory.

'I must admit, Simon,' Viktor said with a sneer, 'you put up quite the fight. But all good things must come to an end, and so must our little bout.'

Simon clenched his fists, digging deep for the strength to rise once more. He must not give in to the pain and exhaustion now. Lives depended on him, and he couldn't let Viktor's reign of terror engulf the world.

In a moment of sheer determination, Simon's indominable will shone forth and he called upon his Fallen Ring: *We either fall today, and you are claimed by Viktor, or, through our shared blood, sweat and tears, we rise together and decide our own fate.*

Steeling himself, he embraced the stillness within, tapping into an unparalleled inner strength he had never felt before. Time seemed to slow down as he focused on Viktor, his senses heightening and his mind becoming razor-sharp. With tai-chi-like movements, he leaped from the splintered cabin, planting himself firmly before Viktor.

Viktor stepped forward and launched another ferocious attack, deftly blocked by Simon, who parried the strikes. Moving with an otherworldly grace, Simon dodged with precision and countered with surprising force. He had become one with the Fallen Ring, a conduit of raw energy. His violet eyes burned brighter than ever; he had reached a new height of power.

Astonishment flickered in Viktor's eyes as Simon's renewed vigour overwhelmed him. The tide of the battle had turned, and it was now Viktor who struggled to keep up with Simon's relentless assault. With every strike and parry, Simon's resolve grew stronger. He could sense the fear in Viktor. Now was the time for him to put an end to this once and for all. But killing Viktor would make him no better than his adversary.

'You had a choice, Simon!' Viktor spat, his voice filled with bitterness. 'But you chose the weak path, the path of restraint. You could have been invincible alongside me.'

Simon's eyes blazed with defiance. 'No, Viktor. I am not on the path of the weak. I am on a path of continuous improvement. I will never become a slave to the darkness like you.'

In a final desperate attempt, Viktor lunged at Simon, hoping to catch him off guard. But Simon had reached a new level of power and understanding. Finally, he had embraced the Fallen Ring's inner core and channelled its energy for the greater good. With precision and strength, he seized the moment, overpowering Viktor and disorientating him with a swift series of strikes to his face and body. The weakened green figure stumbled backwards and fell onto his knees, defeated and at Simon's mercy.

Viktor's eyes glinted with hatred and desperation. 'If you don't kill me now, I'll never stop. I'll keep coming back ... until I crush you!'

Simon hesitated for a moment, contemplating the weight of his decision. He could end Viktor's reign here and now, eliminating his rival entirely. But in his heart, he knew he couldn't become what Viktor was – a ruthless conqueror. With a measured breath, he chose a different path.

Tapping deep into his shared bond with the silver Ring, he searched for a solution. *We need not kill him, Simon. Instead, we can lock him far away*, whispered the Ring in his mind. That was it. He would not kill Viktor; instead, he would banish him into a different realm – the Shadow

Plane: a bleak and negatively charged dimension parallel to earth. There he would not be able to hurt anybody. Summoning the radiating power deep within, Simon tore a hole in the fabric of reality and transported Viktor through the gateway. In a flash, the portal flickered out, and the tear fused back together again. With his nemesis now neutralised, Simon stood there, breathing heavily.

The storm began to subside, and the air felt calmer. For a moment, everything was still and tranquil. But the serenity was short-lived. Beneath his feet, the ground was trembling. The destruction inflicted by their battle was causing the island to sink. He needed to escape – and fast.

With the last vestiges of his strength, he propelled himself off the island and back to the mainland. Standing on the shore, he watched Piel Island submerge slowly beneath the waters, a mixture of relief and sorrow washing over him. He had won, but the encounter had taken its toll.

He turned from the site of his climactic showdown, his senses alert. The distant rumble of a helicopter's rotors reached his ears. Instinctively, he knew it wasn't there on a casual visit. Flashing searchlights swept across the landscape, signalling an active search. He needed to make himself scarce. The sinking of the island would no doubt become televised news, but it wasn't an event he wished to be a part of. With a sense of urgency, he retreated from the scene, slinking away into the shadows.

Chapter 25

— · —

The moment Simon's head hit the pillow, fatigue and exhaustion overtook him. His eyelids grew heavy, and he drifted off into a dream-like state, an ethereal realm where he found himself standing in an all-white room. The walls glowed with an otherworldly light. It felt surreal yet oddly familiar, as if he had been here before.

A figure emerged from the brilliance, and his heart skipped a beat. It was Cornelius, the old man who had created the Fallen Rings. The memory of their first meeting on the train, and the lucid nature of the experience rushed back to him in a flood of emotions. And here he was, standing before him, exuding an aura of wisdom and unfathomable power. His light-brown eyes held a depth of knowledge that Simon found both comforting and unsettling. Dressed in a sharp grey suit with his dark, silky hair combed back, Cornelius looked as if he hadn't aged a day since their last meeting. Being a superlunary, he projected an image that was beyond impressive, but one that was also to be expected, thought Simon.

'Simon, my young friend.' Cornelius greeted him with a warm smile. 'It's good to see you again.'

'Likewise, Cornelius. I've been wanting to see you again for a long time,' Simon said, delighted to see the old man.

Cornelius nodded knowingly. 'I understand, Simon. I have been away but I've been watching over you from a distance. The power of the Rings is not to be taken lightly, but sometimes the path must be navigated without direct intervention.'

'I get that. But … I really could have used your guidance earlier. There were times when I … felt terrible, completely down. I didn't know what to do, or even if I would make it,' Simon said.

'But you did, didn't you, Simon. Even at your lowest moments, you did not give up on yourself. You got back up and dusted yourself off. You acknowledged the adversity, saw the dangers, but you were still courageous enough to stand and face them, aiming for something far greater,' Cornelius said with a smile, his eyes kind and supportive.

Simon paused, taking in Cornelius's words.

'What about Viktor Nemesis. Couldn't you have taken his Ring away, or stopped himself yourself?'

Cornelius sighed gently. 'There are principles, Simon, even ones by which we must abide. Direct intervention in this case was not an option.'

'But he was so dangerous,' Simon protested, remembering the overwhelming strength of his adversary.

Cornelius nodded, acknowledging the gravity of the situation. 'Indeed, Viktor was a formidable foe, and your encounter was not without risk. But you proved yourself as an exemplary Ring bearer, Simon. You rose above the darkness and found a new balance within yourself. You even achieved a new ability. I'm proud of you for that.'

'Thank you, Cornelius. I needed to hear that.' Imparted with wisdom, Simon looked down, reflecting on his incredible achievements. 'So, when will we meet again?'

'I cannot say, Simon, but I will leave you with this,' Cornelius said, his eyes shining with ancient wisdom. 'Whenever you feel down or dispirited, remember all the people you have saved. All the people you have positively affected. Even if you don't remember them, they surely remember you. I hear their praises in the heavens as they root for you. So be the protector that the world needs and never forget that you are not alone.'

Hearing this, Simon swelled with pride and a newfound sense of purpose and clarity that bolstered his confidence. It was knowledge he would never forget. But one question burned in his mind.

'Cornelius, I've been meaning to ask you ... what happened to James, after he died? Can you tell me where he is now?'

'I thought you might never ask,' said Cornelius with a smile. 'What I can tell you is that your dear friend, James, is in a wonderful place now. And when the time comes, I'm sure you'll both have a lot to talk about.'

Simon sighed with relief, a tear trickling down his face. He would look forward to the day when he could see James again. There really would be a lot to catch up on!

As the dream reached its conclusion, Cornelius placed a hand on Simon's shoulder and a surge of warm energy coursed through his body. It felt like a blessing, a reassurance that he would continue to have guidance from a higher form on his journey. His meeting with Cornelius had been so different to their previous meeting; it was positive, peaceful and uplifting. He wished it had been like this the first time around.

With everything fading around him, Simon awoke and found himself back in his bedroom, the memory of the dream still vivid in his mind. So vivid he could almost feel Cornelius's presence lingering in the air. The silver Ring on his finger even seemed to gleam with a newfound brilliance.

Taking a moment to reflect upon the profound encounter, he realised that something was different about his body. The bruises and injuries from his battle with Viktor were rapidly healing, and a revitalising energy was coursing through him. The Ring had bestowed its healing power upon him once more.

With a newfound sense of resolve and understanding, Simon rested his head back on his pillow, and drifted off into a well-earned slumber.

Chapter 26

Simon walked with vigour and purpose through the crowded halls of the university. The events of the past few days had left him rejuvenated and filled with a renewed sense of determination. The intense battle with Viktor had tapped into an inner strength he didn't know he possessed, and the guidance from his dream with Cornelius had provided him with some much-needed clarity and wisdom.

Reach the dining hall, he paused, a spark of excitement igniting inside him. He scanned the room, searching for Layla. There she was, sitting with a group of friends, her smile radiant as she laughed at something one of her mates was saying. His heart started beating rapidly with nervousness and anticipation as he approached her. Would she still be interested in talking to him after his sudden departure on their last outing? Taking a deep breath, he mustered up the courage to greet her.

'Hey, Layla,' he said, trying to sound casual.

Her face lit up as she turned to him. 'Simon! It's good to see you. How have you been?'

Simon smiled back at her as a weight lifted off his shoulders. 'I'm doing much better, thanks. As a matter of fact, I feel like a new person.'

Layla seemed puzzled by his response, but she didn't press further. Instead, she smiled warmly and said, 'Come with me. I want to show you something.'

Intrigued, Simon followed her as she led him to the university's art block. The art room was quiet and filled with the smell of paint and uncapped creativity. Layla motioned towards an easel covered with a cloth.

'I've been working on this for a while,' she said, excitement dancing in her eyes. 'It's a portrait of you.'

Simon's heart skipped a beat as she pulled away the cloth, revealing the stunning painting. It was him, but not just a simple likeness – Layla had captured something deeper in the brushstrokes, something that made him feel seen in a way he had never been seen before.

'It's incredible,' he said with a gasp, his mouth falling open. 'You're so talented, Layla.'

Her cheeks flushed with pleasure at the compliment. 'Thank you. I'm glad you like it.'

They spent the rest of the day together, talking and laughing as they wandered around the campus. Simon found himself opening up to Layla about the recent events in his life – his goals, fears and doubts. She listened with genuine interest and understanding, offering words of encouragement and support.

As the day turned into evening, they sat down under a tree on the campus green, the setting sun casting a warm glow over them. A sense of peace settled over Simon, a feeling he hadn't experienced in a long time, and it was all because of Layla.

'I never expected to find someone like you,' said Simon, looking into her eyes.

Layla smiled softly. 'And I never expected to find someone like you. You're different, Simon, in the best way possible.'

There was something special between them, an unspoken connection that was growing stronger with every passing moment. He wanted to tell her everything – about the Ring, his alter ego and the battle he'd fought to protect the world. But it wasn't the right time. He didn't want to burden her with his secrets, not yet at least.

As they sat together, he couldn't shake the feeling that the rest of the evening would be spent basking in each other's company, a thought that brought a smile to his lips and a warmth to his heart.

CHAPTER 27

Simon stood atop The Shard, London's iconic skyscraper, gazing out over the sprawling city below. The city lights painted a mesmerising tapestry against the dark canvas of the night sky. The Ring on his finger glowed faintly, resonating with the excitement in his heart. He inhaled deeply with pride. He was the Guardian of the night, a protector of the city. His city. Deep in his mind, the silver Ring's voice whispered, sharing his appreciation of the stunning view. Simon smiled. The ancient artefact had become an integral part of his life. With its power, he was more than just a regular university student, he was a defender of the innocent, a hero in the shadows.

Leaning against The Shard's railing, he let the cool night air brush against his face, invigorating him. It was moments like this that made him feel alive, fully embracing his alter ego. The city hummed with life beneath him, distant sirens blaring, indicating that the police, the firefighters and paramedics, the city's frontline protectors, were out on their own missions.

Unable to resist the call of duty any longer, with a determined look, he leaped off The Shard's rooftop, letting the

Ring's power guide him. In an instant, he was swinging across the buildings, now a blur of motion as he effortlessly navigated the urban jungle.

Bounding over rooftops and gliding through the night, he found a sense of freedom he couldn't find anywhere else. The Ring's voice encouraged him, pushing him to move faster and to become even more agile. He was a nocturnal creature, at one with the shadows, silently watching over the city's slumbering inhabitants.

As the police sirens grew louder, he instinctively moved towards the source of the disturbance, picking up speed. Before he sprang into action, Cornelius's words echoed in his mind: 'I hear their praises in the heavens as they root for you. So be the protector that the world needs and never forget that you are not alone.' He had taken those words to heart. He was not just a man with a Fallen Ring, he was a symbol of hope and courage in the darkness of the night.

ACKNOWLEDGEMENTS

Books are not one-person endeavours. Creating them and getting them out to readers is a commitment that takes dedication. That's why I am so grateful to my editor, my aunt and to all of you who supported and helped make this book possible. I could not have done it without you!

About the Author

Key Dawkins is a writer and author from the UK. Since childhood, he's always wanted to write and publish a book. This is his second one within the young adult and thriller genre, following the first *The Fallen Ring* novella.